I0707600

Alienable Rights

A Political Satire
in which everyone gets screwed

This is a work of adult fiction.

This book contains content of an adult nature. This includes explicit sexual content and characters whose beliefs may be contrary to your religious, political, or world view—I hope. The content is inappropriate and in some cases illegal for readers under the age of 18.

Dedicated to all the people walking in a daze, trying to figure out, "What the hell is happening to our world?"

At last we know! People have been dazed and confused by all the things going on in the US lately. The government shut down. Agents are in the streets. And frogs are on the front lines. Everyone in a Halloween mask. Is it any wonder that no one believes the media? Is it all fake news?

No! It's the aliens. They've landed and they're here to stay in Longview, Kansas.

Satire, parody, and humor, with lots of tentacle sex!

Alienable Rights

A Political Satire
in which everyone gets screwed

Devon Layne

ELDER ROAD BOOKS
LYNNWOOD WA

1
Abduction

IT WAS A DAY like any other in Longview, Kansas. Located in the geographic center of Kansas, you could see both trees in the state. It was also close enough to the geographic center of the United States that it challenged any other town to try to claim the title. That was its only official tourist attraction and might have been the least visited attraction in the country.

If you climbed to the top of the water tower in Longview—as had many high school students, attested by their class numbers on the landmark—with a good pair of binoculars, you could see the Rocky Mountains in the West and the Mississippi River in the East. There was really no reason to look either north toward Nebraska or south toward Oklahoma.

There were many notable sites, much interesting history, and a few eccentric people in this lazy Midwestern town of 3,758 souls. Most of that will be revealed as the story progresses. In its Wild West days as a Cowtown, it was known as the best armed city in America. It was pretty much all farmland in the twenty-first century, mostly wheat, corn, and sorghum. But there wasn't a farmer on the prairie who couldn't shoot straight.

Longview happened to also be a town devoted to the celebration of Halloween. That was its *unofficial* tourist attraction. It was not a children's holiday, but a day when the normally reserved citizens all dressed in outrageous costumes and attracted celebrants from miles around. On that day, the population of Longview doubled.

The legend has it that back in October of 1869 a prairie fire raged so hot and swift that the town was covered in smoke. People feared for their survival and all wore bandanas over their faces so they could breathe. As it happened, two rival gangs of Texans—it's always the Texans—decided to rob the newly opened Butterfield Bank, which was said to have more than $300 in its new Cary safe. They rode into town with their faces covered with bandanas only to find everyone in the bank similarly attired. There were a couple of fistfights that broke out, and when the Texans realized they couldn't tell who was the robber and who was the victim, they retired to the plentiful houses of prostitution where it is said they left more money than they would have gained had they cracked the safe.

And all the time, they were in the company of women without a stitch of clothing on except the masks across their faces. Some of the 'respectable' women of town were thought to have earned a few extra dollars that night and a few of the town fathers enjoyed their neighbors' wives for a small price.

The masks and the lewd behavior had stuck as a part of the last night of October for over 150 years.

None of that would qualify Longview to become the next capital city of the United States of America. It took a far-thinking genius to come up with that idea, and a strange logic to make it so.

It all began on Tuesday, October 28 at the airport in New York, where Darrell Gwinner was impatiently waiting for his flight home to Longview. Of course, there *were* no flights to Longview. Its airport was a grass strip through what used to be Ronnie Plunkett's bean field. He and Patience still lived out there and Ronnie spent his time intently listening to the radio chatter, hoping something would land there.

No, Darrell would have to fly to Kansas City and catch a bus from there to Salina before he could call Stacy to drive out forty-five minutes to pick him up. Of course, it would take her an hour and a half, because everything took longer when you had a three-month-old. Stacy was a fine woman and there were those in Longview who believed he'd married above his station. Including him.

His nineteen-year-old wife was a real looker and proved to be real fertile when she caught the baby batter just a few weeks after they were married. Darrell had breathed a sigh of relief at that. Not that she'd gotten pregnant so easily, but that with the amount of messing around they'd done for a year before they got married, she hadn't gotten pregnant before. She'd at least managed to finish high school first.

Darrell was a pretty good catch for the girl, too. He'd gone to college in Lawrence and got a job with the Midwest Tillage Exchange. He brokered grain sales from the heartland all over the world. That's why he was in New York City, a trip that had taken him all day Sunday to be there for a four-hour meeting with the honchos Monday, before being able to fly back to the Midwest. Of course, there was no flight that late on Monday, so he was at the airport way too early Tuesday morning to be free of the hangover from dinner with his boss the night before.

Darrell was a big promoter of his little town of Longview, so when he got the job and they suggested he would want to live in Chicago, he sold the Midwest Tillage Exchange executives on the idea that Longview was smackdab in the middle of the richest farmland in the country and he should be close to where the crops were. To his surprise, they agreed and he went back to his hometown to set up a branch office of the Exchange.

He needed some help in the little office on Wyatt Avenue downtown. He'd hired Stacy part-time while she was still in high school and they'd started screwing long before she graduated. She'd been justifiably upset when she had to quit the job in order to have and care for the baby and Darrell hired another slut from the same high school. Kristin was just a year younger than Stacy.

Darrell hadn't fooled around with Kristin, though. Too much. And realizing how easily Stacy caught, he was always careful to use protection.

Just as he'd done in New York when his boss pointed out a hooker outside Darrell's hotel and handed him $500 to 'go have a good time.' He could have taken the $500 home as a badly needed bonus, but he was pretty drunk by that time and that hooker looked pretty fine. Before she left, she'd managed to pull another $200 from his wallet, so Darrell had to hit a cash machine in the morning in order to get home. But what he remembered was a hell of a good time before she left.

So, there he was, at the airport waiting for a flight to Kansas City that was already delayed. They said weather conditions in the fly-over states were delaying flights, but Darrell knew that they were still looking for a pilot willing to fly to Kansas Fucking City. Nobody really went there willingly.

"Coffee? Like, just coffee?" the girl at the coffee counter asked. "Like a latte? Cappuccino? Macchiato?"

"Can I just get a cup of black coffee?" Darrell asked, rubbing his throbbing head.

"Arnold! Do we have black coffee?" she called to the other worker behind the counter.

"Oh, geez! Midwesterners, I bet. Make a single shot Americano. Charge a quarter less than the regular Americano."

"But the regular has two…"

"You heard me!"

"Yes, sir. That'll be $6.50. I'll make it for you right away," she said, smiling at Darrell. He handed her a ten-dollar bill and she thanked him. She didn't offer him change.

A few minutes later, he took his first sip of the weak-ass coffee she served him. This wasn't going to help his hangover much. Sarah Lee's coffee, back in Longview, could cure a hangover in two sips.

He sat in the waiting area and waited. His flight was posted as being delayed an hour. He dropped his chin to his chest and dozed off, starting himself awake each time his coffee cup started to tip into his lap.

When his flight was finally ready for boarding, he joined the crush of people in his section as they jockeyed for position in the boarding line. He looked at his seat assignment and discovered he was right in the middle of the widebody jet. Almost. There were three seats to his right, occupied by a man, a woman, and a three-year-old who was already unhappy about sitting next to the icky man. The seat on his left, next to the aisle, remained unoccupied until the last second. Darrell had prepared to move to it when a woman stopped and set a computer bag down on the seat. She reached overhead to try to shove a pack in the bin, to no avail.

"Excuse me." she said, dropping down to face Darrell, who had been looking at a very short skirt and lovely pair of legs. "Could I beg of you to put my computer bag under the seat in front of you so I can put my pack under this seat? I promise, it will only be for takeoff and landing. I will take it as soon as we can get our bags out. I just can't believe they don't allow enough room for decent carry-on bags."

"Um… Oh… Uh…. Sure, I guess. Just for takeoff," Darrell said, accepting the computer bag from her. He wedged it in under the seat in front of him. He didn't have anything there because he'd put both his bags in the overhead bin. Served him right, he guessed.

"I'm Janelle Cummbridge," the woman said as soon as she was seated and buckled in. "What a cattle car, right?" She looked to be about Darrell's age. Maybe twenty-five.

"I guess. We don't run much cattle anymore where I'm from. Darrell Gwinner," he said offering his hand. She took it and didn't let go, pretending to examine it closely as she stroked his palm with her thumb.

"Are you from Missouri?" she asked.

"Kansas," he said.

"It's a toss-up," she said. "No booze in Kansas and no sex in Missouri."

"What?"

"Sorry, I'm a… performer. You know. Exotic dancer is the polite word. I live in Missouri, so I can get a drink when I want. But I work in Kansas. You wouldn't believe the rules they have for dancers in Missouri. It's the 'Show me—not much' state. Do you know how much the adhesive on pasties irritates my sensitive bits? I work at a club on the south Johnson County Line in Kansas if you're ever there." She lowered her voice, suddenly concerned she could be overheard. The three-year-old was staring at them. "I'll show you *everything!*" she whispered.

"That sounds… like a reason to spend an extra day in Kansas City," Darrell said.

"Well, I won't work tonight. Unless you call me for a private performance. I'll be at the club tomorrow."

Darrell did a quick calculation of how much money he had in his wallet and figured he could make another stop at an ATM.

"Give me your number and I'll call. Recommend any convenient place to stay?"

"Crowne Plaza is always nice. I like going there."

"I'll give them a call as soon as we land," he said.

While they'd been talking, the plane had taken off and was

banking around to head west. In a few minutes the seatbelt sign was turned off and they got more comfortable, putting the armrest between their seats up out of the way. Janelle asked for her computer bag.

"Want to be in one of my OF vids?" she asked. "I mean we won't show anything here, just us having a good time on the plane. Oh! Here comes the drink cart."

They both asked for whiskey. Darrell decided to have a coffee, too. Janelle opened her tablet and propped it on the tray table.

"Here I am with my new friend DG," she said when she'd hit the record button. "We're getting to know each other really well." She leaned against Darrell and he put his arm around her, smiling at the camera. He could see their image on the screen and laughed because the words on his logo were backwards. "Say something, DG."

"I found something here that will make this flight worthwhile!" he said, giving her a squeeze. She raised her glass and they toasted each other.

Over the next hour, they chatted, sneaked little kisses, and had another drink. Darrell wasn't completely a country bumpkin. He'd gone to college in Lawrence and knew pretty well what was available on the internet. He could tell an Only Fans performer when he met her. If she was willing to "show everything," he had no difficulty playing with her on camera. After they'd finished their second round of drinks, Janelle leaned close to him.

"I have to go tinkle. You know, usually girls go together, but there aren't any girls here. Want to come with me?" she asked.

"I would hate to think of you having to go all alone," he said.

They slipped out of their seats and made their way down the aisle toward the restrooms. It was only eleven-thirty in the morning. The meal service had not yet begun and people were watching movies, playing games, and working on their computers or cell phones. Janelle stopped in front of a bank of toilets. One opened, but she ignored it.

"This one," she said, when the next door opened.

"Why this one and not the first one that opened," he asked.

"This one is marked as a changing room. It has a little more room in it than the others. We'll just have to hope no babies are pooping their pants right now," she giggled.

She pulled down her panties and sat on the toilet, pulling Darrell toward her. She unzipped his fly and fished out his cock. He didn't think he was overly big, but Janelle sounded appreciative.

"I really do have to pee," she explained as he heard the sound of water in the toilet. "But there's room for some fun when I'm done."

Darrell noticed that she brought the tablet with her into the tiny restroom and propped it on the sink before she sucked his cock into her mouth. It felt like she'd done this before. A lot. She was an expert at blowjobs, in Darrell's humble opinion. She patted herself with a bit of toilet paper and stood to close the lid and press the flush button.

"It's easiest if I bend over the changing table," she said. "Here. Put this on." She handed him a condom and he ripped it open to apply before slotting himself into her pussy and pushing.

Janelle pulled the tablet toward her and started talking to the camera.

"Can you believe we're doing this on the plane at something like 35,000 feet above the ground? That's like the six-mile-high club! If you don't believe we're really doing this, take a look!"

She pushed the tablet down between her legs so the camera could look at him plowing her welcoming furrow.

"Fuck, yes! I think I'm going to cum. Are you going to cum, DG?"

"Yeah. Fuck, Janelle. I'm going to cum in your pussy!" Darrell exclaimed.

He fulfilled his end of that deal and thought he could feel Janelle spasming around his cock as well. There was a little jolt as the whole plane shuddered, but the fasten seatbelt sign didn't come on, so they didn't worry about it.

"I don't usually kiss guys I record with," Janelle said as she turned around, pulling him out of her. She pressed her lips to his and her tongue into his mouth. "That was really good. Honestly, I don't usually cum when I do this, but this time… Damn, DG! I'm looking forward to tonight."

Darrell stripped off the rubber and put it in the waste bin, then took his turn to pee and clean out his pipes a little. He tucked himself back into his trousers. Then he pulled Janelle to him to kiss thoroughly again.

"We've been in here a while," she said. "Someone probably has to use it by now."

She opened the door a crack and thrust the tablet out, looking at the screen, then she opened the door wide. Darrell followed her out of the toilet and looked up and down the aisle. Everyone on the plane was asleep. It was extremely quiet. The lights had been dimmed as well.

"Did it become night while we were fucking?" Darrell asked.

"I don't think so. This is strange."

"Oh! You're awake. You should be asleep," a flight attendant said, approaching them in the aisle.

Darrell was certain he saw something retract into the sleeve of her uniform and a hand replace it.

"You're…" he began.

"Yes. You saw me. Ordinarily we'd keep that for later in the adventure, but you're the first ones to see who your abductors are," the flight attendant said. She didn't look at all threatening. "So, you're the only ones awake. Do you want to watch the show or go to sleep with the others?"

Darrell took a quick glance at Janelle and saw she was still recording.

"If it's all the same with you, we'd like to watch," Darrell said. "We're really being abducted by aliens?"

"Oh, yeah. Um… Let me see." She began unbuttoning her blouse and pulling it open. Beneath they saw green boobs. A tentacle reached out from under her arm. She stroked Darrell's face and he found it to be very sensual.

"Oh, yeah!" Janelle said. "I have one of your dildos. I've always wondered what it would be like to have a live tentacle do me. Will you?"

"You're just my type," the flight attendant said, withdrawing her tentacle and buttoning her blouse again. "First, though, I have duties regarding docking the plane in our ship."

"Do we need to sit down?" Darrell asked.

"Hah! No. Come up to the flight deck where you can see better. Once the ship took control, we were guaranteed a smooth ride. No one needs a seatbelt."

She opened the door to the flight deck and ushered them inside. In the captain's chair on the left, a large green man sat, relaxing with a copy of *Men's World* grasped between his tentacles. He looked up at them.

"Hey, Haro," the flight attendant said. "These guys were having sex and missed the knockout party. They'd like to watch. Okay?"

"Oh, sure. You guys aren't too freaked out?" he asked.

"No, no. It's cool," Darrell said. Maybe two whiskeys and a cum had distorted his senses a little. "You do this often?"

"That's an old pickup line," said the flight attendant. "I think I heard it the first time back, oh, a hundred of your years ago."

"You're that old?" Janelle asked, looking at the apparently naked captain.

The copilot was also naked with tentacles instead of hands. Otherwise they looked almost human. Apparently, they were somewhat psychic.

"We keep a human shape on most of the time because it helps us with the language and with not frightening the babies," the flight attendant said.

Janelle had moved automatically a little closer to the captain. He reached out and invited her onto his lap. She hiked up her skirt and pulled down her panties before she accepted his invitation to straddle his lap. He opened his trousers.

"You don't have, like, a dick," she said facing him.

"Oh, you'll like this," he said. "We keep those organs concealed until needed."

Janelle felt something tickling at her nether lips until it found her opening. Then it seemed to crawl up inside her.

"Oh! Nice! A little skinny, but… Oh!"

The appendage that made its way into her body began to grow and expand until she thought she'd burst.

"Oh, DG! You were great, but this is something else!"

Darrell scarcely had a chance to notice. The flight attendant had also stripped. She had a green human face and torso, but tentacles for arms and legs. He reached out and squeezed her boobs. They seemed perfect.

"Human men are so much easier to handle if they're faced with a pair of boobs," the flight attendant said. "But you've never felt anything like this!"

She got him out of his trousers and underwear and stroked his cock with a tentacle that seemed to wrap around him and caress every nerve in his penis. Then she settled onto his erection with her midsection. That's all Darrell could call it because he hadn't actually seen what his cock was sinking into. All he knew was that whatever it was, it was better than any pussy, mouth, or ass he'd ever been in. It seemed made to draw the essence of his life right out his dick. When he erupted in her, he could hear Janelle loudly declaring her pleasure as well.

He glanced over and saw the copilot had planted his sex appendage in her ass and she had another tentacle in her mouth. Janelle seemed in a constant state of orgasm. By that time, Darrell was rising to another cum as well.

"Shit! I didn't use a condom!" he said while the last spurts were still leaving his dick.

"Don't worry. We haven't found a way to breed with humans and we've tested for all communicable diseases. Nothing seems to transfer one way or the other. I'm Zeta, by the way."

"Yeah. Um… Darrell," he stammered. "Is our whole stay with you going to be like this, or are we going to get eaten by morning?" He thought his wits were returning slowly.

"Oh, no. We don't eat people. We plan to take over your planet, not kill it. You people have done a royal job of fucking things up. We figured if we don't move soon, there won't be a planet left to save."

"Save the planet. Fuck an alien," Janelle gasped when the appendage was removed from her mouth and throat. She watched it, fascinated, as it shrank back into the pilot's body.

"You two are all right," Haro, the captain, said. He clenched a little and Janelle felt something inside that drove her over the cliff again. "We could use a couple of people to help us plan the invasion. What do you say?"

"You're really going to save the planet?" Darrell asked.

"And make sure you get all the fucking you could want while we do it," Zeta said.

"I'm in," he said.

"Yeah. You sure are. Let me kiss you a little. It will help you cum again."

The face, mouth, and tongue were human enough for Darrell. He kissed her and by the time they parted for air, he was pumping into her again.

2
Fake News

"DC Air flight 1427 from New York to Kansas City disappeared from radar and radio contact at exactly noon Eastern Standard Time. The last known location of the flight was just south of Wheeling, West Virginia," said the news broadcast. "Search planes have been dispatched and are criss-crossing the area looking for any sign of the downed aircraft. As a precaution, Air Force fighter jets are circling the area, alert for any sign of illegal activity. If you have any information as to the whereabouts of the missing aircraft, please call the number at the bottom of your screen immediately."

"WELL, SHIT, BABY BOY. That's your daddy's flight. Don't think badly of me. I'm going to drop you off at Granny and PopPop's for a while until we get this sorted out. I might have to drive to West Virginia to identify his body," Stacy said.

And if it was the worst, she might not come back.

THE SECURITY COUNCIL was waiting for the president when he came off the eighteenth green at his private golf course Wednesday morning. Secret Service agents surrounded him and the Middle Eastern prince he was golfing with. The president bid his guest farewell and the prince's guards met him as they went to his motorcade.

Bob Sinclair was the only member of the Security Council the president trusted, so the others were cut off from him by the Secret Service.

"It's time for dinner, Bob. Whatever it is, it can wait until we get inside and have food in front of us."

"Yes, sir. Of course, sir," Bob answered nervously, glancing at the sky. It would be better to get inside as quickly as possible. It was obvious the president wasn't in a good mood and a glance at one of the agents got a mouthed, "He lost." That explained things.

Once they were inside and seated at the president's long dining table, Bob was given clearance to talk. None of the president's family nor other advisors were present for the meal. The president's gold plate was twice the size of Bob's plastic one and had twice the amount of food. He started eating quickly as Bob began his story.

"Sir, it's about the plane that went missing at noon yesterday."

"Find the wreckage?"

"No, sir. There is no sign it disassembled. We believe it was captured by aliens."

"Shoot it down!"

"We don't know where they took it."

"Get Homeland Security and Border Control on it. Deploy ICE. They're supposed to keep illegal aliens out of our country. Don't even say anything to the public. Divert the plane straight to El Salvador. Better yet, send them to Uganda."

"Sir, we don't think it was aliens from Mexico, Canada, or China. We're talking about space aliens."

The president spat a mouthful of food across the table as he choked out a laugh.

"Good one, Bob. That's why I like to keep you around. You're always entertaining."

"I'm serious, sir," Bob said. "A witness saw the plane overhead and said it suddenly just vanished. He was sure he could see a shadow of it as it ascended into heaven."

"Which is it? God or aliens?" the president pounced.

"It's the only thing that was taken today, so we have to believe God wasn't involved. You and I wouldn't be here if it was the rapture."

"Right. But aliens don't exist. It's either Antifa or Black Lives Matter."

"Those were five years ago, sir."

"You can't trust the liberals!"

"Of course not, sir. We think the threat is real."

"Are you trying to irritate me, Bob? Get out of my dining room!"

Bob left and went to report the meeting, such as it was, to the rest of the council.

"I've said it before and I'll say it again. There is no such thing as space aliens," the president posted on his social media account.

"Space aliens are a product of artificial intelligence controlled by the liberal media," he doubled down.

"Anything you hear about space aliens is fake news. We believe CNN is at the heart of this misinformation."

Of course, his posts were the first anyone had heard of a threat from space aliens, including CNN.

"Has the president lost it?" asked a media post, quoting the president's messages.

By morning, though, when the country was waking up to their cell phones and looking at them through bleary eyes, the president's posts had all been removed. The rabid discussion on the internet and in the morning news, however, was in full bloom.

"Pentagon refuses to deny invasion by space aliens!" screamed one headline.

"Air Force reportedly on alert for invasion from space."

"No evidence," stated a banner across responses and reposts that included screenshots of the president's tweets. The social media AIs worked overtime to hide the posts. Everything that talked about aliens, however, could not be removed.

UFO Today, a publication that mimicked a national newspaper, had the most extensive article on the subject, including quotes from prominent scientists.

> *We should not be surprised at the sudden furor raised about comments that seemed to indicate the president was aware of alien activity in our airspace. We at UFO Today have known about this activity for several years. The reluctance of the government to confirm the story, originally credited to the president in posts that have since been removed, is the same that we have encountered over the years when we attempted an investigation.*
>
> *Word that another aircraft has disappeared, this time from directly over US airspace rather than the fabled Bermuda Triangle, has sparked more rumors of alien contact. Whether these rumors are true or not, we can't say. But the disappearance of DC Air flight 1427 has all the same hallmarks as other historic flights that have vanished without a trace.*
>
> *As early as 1932, a US troop transport plane flying from Guam to the Philippines disappeared with 90 troops on*

board. There was no signal from the plane and no wreckage was ever found. The crew of a Liberian tanker plying the waters on that route reported seeing an intensely luminous light in the sky. Did the plane blow up, or was it snatched by a powerful beam?

In 1974, an unscheduled Argentine troop transport with three crew and 21 passengers disappeared. Just vanished. No trace of the aircraft or the people on it was ever found.

Is it always people? No. The missing aircraft and ships seem to have all kinds of cultural artifacts aboard. For example, a cargo flight from Tokyo to Rio with only six people aboard disappeared without a trace. The plane vanished with 153 rare paintings valued at over $1.2 million!

What made the Bermuda Triangle famous? The triangle extends from southern Florida, to Bermuda, to Puerto Rico. Within that region, ships with goods and passengers had long been known to disappear. On December 5, 1945, Flight 19, a group of five Navy fighters two hours into a training mission out of Fort Lauderdale reported a compass malfunctioning and the leader was not sure where they were. All five aircraft and the fourteen men on them were never seen nor heard from again.

A flight over Pakistan carrying 54 passengers disappeared in 1989.

The largest search effort for a missing aircraft in history took place in 2014 when Malaysia Airlines Flight 370 disappeared without a trace on its flight from Kuala Lumpur to Beijing. It vanished from clear skies early in the morning on March second. No flashes or crew distress signals. The plane, its 239 crew and passengers, and radio signals just vanished.

So, now we add DC Air Flight 1427 from New York to Kansas City with 369 passengers and crew. Possibly the largest single abduction in history, the flight vanished over West Virginia yesterday. Is it any wonder that people—maybe even the president—speculated alien interference?

An eye witness claimed the plane was overhead one moment and the next, it was gone. The plane vanished so quickly, said the witness, that for a minute it left its shadow still flying up toward the heavens.

Perhaps the aliens responsible for this abduction are angels. And maybe this time, we'll find out!

Somewhere south of Wheeling, West Virginia, Harlan Graves was trying to follow the directions of the only witness to the disappearance of DC Air Flight 1427. The FAA investigator looked at the scribbled map on a diner placemat and scratched his head.

"Why couldn't he have given me GPS coordinates?" Harlan mumbled. "There. That must be where Jim Bob's cattle broke through the hedge back in 1999. Could he have been more cryptic? It's the only thing I could call a hedge I've seen in five miles. Now, there should be a two-track lane off to the right. What the fuck was that guy doing out here anyway?"

Harlan crept forward, finally seeing what might pass for a two-track lane. It was more like two footpaths running parallel to each other, but he thought he could keep the tires of his Bronco in the worn spots. He turned in and made his way down the lane with hawthorn branches and blackberry bushes scratching along the sides. The witness had been out here right at noon, stretched out in the bed of his truck having a smoke and a little drink before he went home from work. Harlan couldn't imagine navigating this path in the dark. The witness said he'd made the stop on his way home from the night shift at a chicken rendering plant.

All Harlan needed to find was one little scrap of anything that might look like it came off an airplane. Evidence of a crash. Then he could call in the NTSB and get them to take over the investigation. He'd tried that once already.

"You lost an airplane off of radar, but there's no sign of a crash. You had helicopters circling the area out ten miles from the supposed site and still no evidence of a crash," Millie MacDonald at NTSB had told him. "We investigate crashes, Harlan. Show me a goddam crash site and we'll get right at investigating."

The FAA had been all over the relevant data. The plane was on the radar and in radio contact until exactly noon. Then nothing. No sign of any equipment failures at any of the tracking stations. It was just there and then it wasn't. And only this yahoo from the sticks of West-By-God Virginia had professed to have seen anything.

The underbrush became less dense and the trees began to part. Harlan had hopes that he could turn around somewhere soon and wouldn't have to back down the lane in order to leave—and that none of the spiky thorns had embedded itself in a tire. Then he came out of the woods into a clearing. A little shack sat in the middle and the track went around it and back out the way he'd come.

As he came back to what he decided to call the front of the shack, he was confronted by a woman with a shotgun leveled at him. He stopped the Bronco and got out, holding his hands high, thankful that he'd heard no dogs barking.

"I come in peace!" he called, wondering if he sounded like a pioneer talking to natives, just before he started shooting them down.

"Ye-ah. Evbdy wanna piece. You brin money?"

Harlan paused and considered.

"How much money?"

"Fify dolla."

"Yeah. I can do that."

Thinking he'd just stumbled on a private place and was being shaken down, he made the quick decision to just pony up and get out. Or maybe he was buying a pint of the local hooch. As he fished money out of his pocket, he decided to investigate as well.

"I'm looking into an airplane crash," he said. "Yesterday at noon. You see or hear anything?" he asked handing over the money. "Can I get a receipt for that?"

"Yo ain' fum he'bout. Jes come inside and take yo close off."

"I… what?" She kept the shotgun pointed at him and herded him into the little shack. Thankfully, it was pretty clean. Sparsely furnished, with a mattress on the floor that was neatly made up into a bed.

"Tak m'off," she demanded.

So, he wasn't going to get any information out of this trip one way or another. And apparently no moonshine either.

"I'll just go."

She raised the shotgun to her shoulder.

"Stee-rip!" she commanded.

Harlan was not a policeman nor a Marine. He wasn't trained in self-defense or martial arts. He'd held a desk job all his adult life and doubted he could even walk back to the highway without having a heart attack. He began removing his clothes and slowly laying them on a chair near the bed.

"Lay down," she said.

He did as he was told. Then she set the shotgun aside and with a quick flick of a couple of buttons, let her dress fall to the floor before she jumped on him. He was surprised at the beauty of the woman in front of him. She had big full breasts with rosy nipples. The bandana was thrown from her head, loosing a cascade of red hair. It matched the hair around her cunt, as far as he could tell. He hadn't been close to a naked woman in a while and his body began to instantly react.

"Thata way I like it," she said as she quickly stuffed him into her pussy before he was completely hard. He kept growing. "Ye-ah. Like home. Make it grow! Make it grow!"

Harlan would not have thought he would respond to the demands of the backwoods woman, but his body had other ideas. It felt like her pussy was sucking on him and stroking him better than any blowjob he'd ever had. His cock increased in all dimensions as he began to thrust up into her. He filled his hands with her big tits and let go of all his inhibitions. If she was offering sex for the fifty dollars he'd paid her, he would simply take it as a good transaction.

"I've never felt anything like this," he moaned as her insides caressed his wood with a sensuousness he was not expecting.

He'd heard of artificial pussies he could buy that were purported to milk the cream from his cock, but had never actually bought one. He'd followed enough links, though—just to investigate—that his social media feeds were filled with advertisements for them.

"Yo like dis eben mo," she said. She reached behind her and slid her hand under his balls. Then he could feel her finger edging its way between his ass cheeks to his anus.

"What? You're… Sweet Jesus! No one ever stuck her finger up there before!"

Her finger slid smoothly into his ass and began pumping in and out. It curled forward a bit and began scratching at his rectum right where he was tightening up to fire semen. She hit his prostate and Harlan came so hard he passed out.

When he woke up, she was dressed and sitting in the chair with the shotgun across her lap. His clothes were on the bed next to him. He started to dress.

"Ya go now," she said.

"You… uh…Yesterday at noon… Did you see an airplane disappear from the sky?"

He was barely dressed and she was shoving him outside without letting him tie his shoes. She raised her shotgun and Harlan instinctively ducked, but she kept swinging it until it pointed almost straight up. She pulled the trigger and the shot echoed all around them.

"Right dere. Cem 'cross fum o'er dere. Right dere, it wen bye-bye."

"Just disappeared or you shot it?"

"Alens took it."

"Alens? Aliens?" he asked.

"Dey all roun he-ah. Neva know wen yo talka one."

She turned and went back into her shack. Harlan thought of following her, but thought of the shotgun and decided to leave. There was no crash debris.

By the time he got off the two-track lane, his Bronco was scratched up on both sides and he was totally bewildered. He considered returning to see the backwoods whore. He'd never had sex like that. Yes, it was quick, but so powerful it had knocked him out. He knew he had a couple hundred more dollars in his pocket and at fifty dollars a lay he could probably die happy.

He pulled to the side of the road and looked at the map the witness had given him. He couldn't make heads or tails of it. He wasn't even sure he had it right side up. He'd never find that shack again!

He drove back to Washington reliving that fuck over and over in his mind. By the time he reached his apartment, he was sure of his course of action.

He called Millie.

"Don't think any of this means I'm going to take over your investigation, Harlan," Millie said as she led him into her apartment. Harlan was a little intimidated because it was much nicer than his. They'd been out to dinner and when Harlan suggested he'd like to come up to her place, she'd shrugged and nodded. That had never happened on their dates before.

"Who cares about any fucking investigation," Harlan growled. "I want you, Millie."

He'd been more than half hard all evening and Millie was feeling a new sense of command from Harlan.

"Oh, Harlan! You've never been so manly before. I'm right here, baby. You want me; you got me."

"Oh, Millie. I'm too old to be going out hunting for pussy on weekends. I want a woman I can have any time I want her. I want you, Millie. You!"

"Let me get that latch, Harlan."

She deftly unhooked her bra and shrugged out of it. Harlan fell to her breasts like a starved man. Millie was a fine-looking woman. He'd never seen her like this before. On their previous dates, she kept her normal business suit on and he'd never been in her apartment before. She moaned as he sucked and flicked her nipples with his tongue. He found the zipper on her skirt.

"I thought you had me in the friend-zone all this time. Oh, Harlan, I love how dominant you're being. Just put me anywhere in any position you want. I haven't had anything like this in way too long," Millie panted.

He pushed her back on the bed and stripped out of his clothes, forgetting about his socks. Then he pulled at her pantyhose until they rolled down her butt and her legs. He grabbed her panties and pulled them down before diving face-first into her pussy.

"Oh, baby! Yes! Lick me up! I love your tongue. And your fingers! You're better than Julie! I'm ready, baby. I'm ready for you."

Harlan hadn't had much experience in orally satisfying a woman, so he assumed telling him she was ready meant he'd succeeded in whatever he was supposed to be doing between her legs and he rushed to her opening with his cock, thrusting it in. *Who the hell was Julie? Should I be worried or excited?* It was a single smooth motion and he felt the delicious sensation of a woman's pussy enveloping his dick for the second time that day. No, Millie wasn't quite milking him like the backwoods ho had, but it was a real live woman who was welcoming him into her body. After a few thrusts at each other, she gave him a push and rolled over on top of him. Millie was more active and athletic than her normal business attire revealed. Bouncing on him with her boobs bobbing up and down was an inspiration to Harlan and he got even more active.

Millie sank down on him to his full length and then began to turn around without losing his erection in her pussy. Facing his feet, she continued to bounce up and down on his cock as he watched and held her beautiful ass in his hands. Then Millie leaned forward a little and began pushing her hand under his balls and toward his anus.

Until earlier that day, Harlan had never known there was pleasure to be had by having a woman push a finger into his butt. Millie's felt more slender than the backwoods woman, but it was still stimulating.

Then Harlan had a sudden inspiration. If it felt good to him, it probably would feel good to her, too. He licked a digit and insinuated it between Millie's cheeks. As soon as he touched her anus, it was like Millie shifted into high gear and began pounding down on his cock while thrusting her ass back against his finger slowly sinking into her butt. She kept up the stimulation on his backside as well and in a few minutes, they both climbed so high up their climax scale that they shorted out and collapsed.

As they slowly regained consciousness, Harlan saw Millie's ass in front of him. It was a sight he determined he was going to see often. Who needed a backwoods whore?

3
A Little Plumbing

OSWALD KENNEDY HAD THE best collection of firearms in Longview County. He also had enough supplies in his little compound to last a year. His neighbors had complained about the eight-foot-tall brick wall he'd built around his compound, but there was no zoning law against it. He'd put iron gates at the only entrance and broken glass along the top. No one would have cared if his compound wasn't right on Oak Street, a block from the center of town.

He only came out of the compound once a week to have coffee at Sarah Lee's Diner, and pick up groceries for the week. Groceries because he had a weakness for good steaks and taking them out of his freezer just wasn't the same as getting them fresh from the butcher. Coffee at Sarah Lee's so he could keep up with the current gossip—or rather news.

So, Thursday morning, October 30th, found him sipping the strong black coffee Sarah Lee served for fifty cents a cup, fifty cents a refill, fifty cents for a warm-up, and fifty cents for just a little more. He listened to the tales the locals were passing around. Oswald didn't have a television, radio, or computer because he didn't want to be subject to all that fake news and that was how the AIs spied on you. He didn't much like any of his neighbors, but he trusted them. Unreasonably, since most of them were passing on news they'd read in memes on social media.

"Nobody here would care about it at all if Stacy Gwinner hadn't said her husband was on that flight. I even wonder if that was true," Bert Beeson said. As mayor of the town of Longview, he easily commanded attention from the other coffee drinkers—half of whom had come in from surrounding farms to get the morning mail at the post office.

"I think she was just using the story to get her truck upgraded," Lyle Staudinger said. "She went into Rick Paulson's to get that old F150 serviced so it would be ready to take her to West Virginia if the government called to have her identify the body. He's such a sap. He put four new tires on it, replaced her broken taillight, changed the oil, sparkplugs, filters, and topped up the coolant for her. You know, all she has to do is pretend she's breastfeeding that kid of hers and guys drool over her tits."

"No. It's for real. Darrell's receptionist, Kristin, over at the Exchange, said Stacy was waiting at the office yesterday when the airline called her and told her they didn't know what happened, but her husband was confirmed to have been on that flight," Don Randall said. As Stacy's father he didn't like hearing negative things about his daughter, but he was a realist and knew his daughter's reputation well. "Besides, she dumped little Cray off with Bea and me so she could leave at a moment's notice."

"Or so she could make a few fast bucks to pay for the trip," one of the guys at another table whispered.

Don pretended he didn't hear. Oswald took notice. He'd always had a thing for Stacy. Back when she was in high school, she always walked home past his compound. She'd stop almost every day to adjust her books or tie her shoes. She always stopped right in front of his security camera.

"I did some research of my own," Bert said, meaning he'd done a Google search. "These aliens have been around for years. Goes back before Area 51."

"Why we never hear about 'em?"

"They're masters of disguise. Can pass themselves off as completely human. Maybe even as dogs and cats. Secret government records show 100,000 of them were deported with other illegal aliens in the past six months, but they never made it to the prisons down south. Just disappeared."

"There ain't none of them around here," Oswald said. "I helped ICE round up all the aliens in the county back in July. We shipped out sixteen of them."

"Yeah, well one was my brother-in-law," Lyle said. "He wasn't illegal."

"I ain't saying no administrative errors were made, but we're a lot safer here now," Oswald insisted.

The truth was Lyle never liked his brother-in-law anyway, so he wasn't that upset. His sister had rolled her eyes and said she should have known better than to spread her legs for a migrant worker. But he did have a green card.

"We need to mobilize the militia," Oswald continued.

"Oswald, we don't have a militia in this town and no one is going to elect you colonel so you can start one," Bert said.

"Well, you just wait. When them aliens are swarming all over town and I'm the only hope, you'll be pounding on my gates to let you in," Oswald said, getting up to leave. "Just see if I open them up for you!" He stormed out of the diner.

"Yeah, yeah," Don muttered. "Who's in charge of the haunted church this year?"

"That would be Patience Plunkett," Bert answered. "We met last night and agreed to do a new scene based on all this alien stuff. Got Kristin Davies to volunteer when it looked like Stacy was going to back out. She's a hot little number. Darrell sure knows how to pick 'em. Don't know who else she's got set up, but I think most of the town is in it, like usual. She's the only one who will know who is who."

"That will be fun," Lyle said. "The corn maze is ready. I expect there will be kids trying it out after school today. Brett did a good job with it."

"How big is it this year?" Bert asked.

"I left ten acres for him to work with. The thing is huge with more places to get lost in than you can imagine. We'll go out Saturday morning and pick the rest so we'll find anyone who's still lost," Lyle laughed.

They kept yammering for a while and eventually, all left before the noon rush came in for lunch.

Normally, Oswald would head straight to Dollar General to get his fresh food. He didn't like to stay away from his compound for too long. He always felt vulnerable, even though he carried a Ruger Security-9mm on his hip. He had other arms that weren't obvious. Kansas had both open and concealed carry without a permit. He wanted people to know he was armed, but not how well.

He hauled his collapsible grocery cart over to Court Avenue and turned north toward 3rd St. He hadn't been over here recently, but he knew the place well. He slipped around the back, looked around, and went up to knock on the door. A minute later, Stacy Gwinner opened the door and looked at him. Oswald caught his breath.

Stacy wore a button-down shirt tied under her boobs and a pair of Daisy Dukes. She was barefoot and looked like a wet dream.

"Mr. Kennedy," she said softly. "I haven't seen you in so long, I thought you didn't love me anymore."

"I didn't want to disturb you with your little one," he said.

"But now?"

"I just stopped by to offer my comfort for your missing husband," Oswald said.

"Yeah, it's a drag. Come on in," Stacy said. Oswald followed her butt cheeks into the kitchen.

"I just wanted to check and see if you were in need of anything. I could help out a little if you had any little tasks your husband would ordinarily take care of," Oswald suggested as she waved him to the table and reached for the pot of coffee she always had brewed.

"Oh, that's so nice of you," Stacy said dramatically. "There might be one or two things you could help with. I'm just so lost without a man in the house."

Stacy laid it on thick, but Oswald lapped it up like a kitten with cream. Now that they were sitting across the table from each other, Stacy's breasts seemed freer under the oversize shirt. Each time she shifted, another portion of one boob or the other was revealed. It was tantalizing.

"You know I'll do whatever I can for you," Oswald said.

"Oh, I know you will!"

Stacy led him upstairs and into the master bedroom.

"The bathroom shower keeps dripping," she complained. "Could you see if it has a leak?"

Oswald was handy. After all, he'd installed all the security at his compound and had handled wiring, plumbing, and even masonry. And it all worked—most of the time. He stepped past Stacy into the bathroom and pulled the curtain aside so he could examine the shower. It was dripping a bit and he pulled out his Leatherman to tighten the screw on the faucet handle a little. The drip stopped. In the process, he bumped against a penis sticking out from the wall.

"Oops!" Stacy said. "I guess I left Momma's little helper in the shower. It works okay, but there's nothing like the real thing."

She was pressed against his back as she reached in to stroke the dildo once. He could feel her boobs pressed against him. He turned slowly and dragged her shirt open wider as she stayed up close to him. It looked like the knot that had been tied under her breasts was completely undone. Her left nipple came fully into view.

"Oh. I think it might be leaking a little here, too," she said, pulling his face down to her tit.

She hadn't actually breastfed Cray, so never leaked from her nipples, but Oswald couldn't have sucked more in earnest if she'd been lactating scotch.

"Yesss," she hissed. "Maybe you could find something else that's leaking and plug it."

He maneuvered her over to her unmade bed and unfastened the short shorts, pushing them down and off her feet. Stacy was completely bald between her legs and the first stroke of his fingers verified that she was, indeed, leaking. He shoved his own pants down and she handed him a condom.

"Better put this on, honey. We don't want a repeat of what happened last time."

Oswald chuckled a little, acknowledging that he knew little Cray was his brat, not Darrell's—an 'accident' just last Halloween. As soon as he was securely wrapped, he leaned forward and pushed his meat into her. Stacy was the best at this. She was active and noisy. He plowed into her repeatedly, bouncing against her pubic bone. He couldn't tell she'd ever had a baby. She was as tight as she'd been when he took her virginity on her way home from school that one time.

He leaned forward and captured one of her nipples in his lips. Then he bit it viciously.

"Yeah! Fuck! I'm cumming! Fuck!" she screamed. With that announcement and the feeling in her pussy, Oswald let go with a flood of his own into the condom. "Oh, baby. You do it so good! Nobody ever bites me like you do. You know, that's why I didn't breastfeed Cray? I mean besides it being gross. I didn't want to lose the feeling in my tits. If I had you any more often, I'd probably still go numb eventually."

"What can I do for you, Stacy?" Oswald asked. He rolled to the side and began fingering her wet slit, seeing if he could bring her to another cum.

"That's nice. You know cash is always welcome. Darrell never even put me on the bank account. I just live on the money he leaves me. And what I can earn, you know."

"I got the grocery money on me," Oswald said. "I'll give you that." He figured he could use a credit card at Dollar General.

"Oh, that's so nice of you. But you know what else I could use even more? With Darrell missing and he's the only one with the key to the gun safe, I feel awful vulnerable here all by myself. What if there *are* aliens? Why, they'd just come in here and have their way with little ol' me. I'd end up having a little green baby. Could you leave me one of your guns?"

"Yeah. I wouldn't want you alone and vulnerable. Why, anybody could just break in and do you. This Ruger is lightweight and packs a punch. I'll leave that with you."

"You're so good to me. Wanna fuck again?"

ELSEWHERE IN TOWN, things were more mundane, but no less intense. For example, in Mrs. Tomlinson's fifth grade class, she was going over the rules for Halloween the next day.

"You may all wear your costumes tomorrow, but you must keep a few things in mind. First, even if your 'character' has a distinct facial characteristic, you may not wear a mask or anything that covers your face to school. This is an important policy so we know who our students are. You don't want an extraterrestrial sneaking into class pretending to be your classmate!"

The students giggled. Mrs. Tomlinson was always entertaining.

"And speaking of spacemen, the school board has set a rule that alien costumes are forbidden," she said.

"Space aliens or illegal aliens?" little Johnny asked.

"Johnny, go immediately to the principal's office. We'll have no reference to undocumented visitors in this class. No. Don't ask another question. Tell the principal what you said."

Johnny grumbled and took his notebook with him to go visit the principal. His book wasn't for notes. He was a pretty good artist and had nearly filled this particular notebook with sketches of what he believed space aliens would look like. He specifically planned to wear a costume based on one of his sketches and had been working on it for two weeks.

Back in class, Mrs. Tomlinson continued her discussion of the rules.

"Now, let's talk about trick-or-treating," she said. "Who can tell me one of the rules for going house to house?" Many hands went up. "Susie?"

"Only go to houses you or your parents know the owners of," she said.

"Very good! Philomena?"

"Don't go to a house with no porchlight on," said the little girl. She hated her name, but at least her parents let her go out on Halloween, unlike Deb's parents. They considered Halloween sinful.

"Be home by nine," offered Lionel. He'd memorized the rule, but because of his dark skin, his parents forbade him from staying out after dark—because you never can tell who might not want a black kid kicking around town at night.

"Don't throw toilet paper at the compound," Becca said.

"Absolutely, do NOT throw toilet paper at the compound. Mr. Kennedy has threatened to shoot anyone who breaches his walls, no matter who or how old! And he's crazy enough to do it," Mrs. Tomlinson said.

"Stay away from the cemetery church," Jenny said.

"Very good. The cemetery church is where adults go for a haunted house and all the people from out of town. It's much too dangerous for children to go where all those nasty strangers are. You can all come to the haunted house in the gym at five. It will be lots of fun."

The kids all groaned.

"Now TELL ME exactly what you said and what your teacher said," Mr. Davies, the principal, said to little Johnny. "You don't need to edit at all. If you are in trouble for something in the classroom, you won't get in more trouble for the same thing by repeating it here."

"Yes, sir," Johnny said respectfully. "Mrs. Tomlinson said the school board has forbidden alien costumes."

Mr. Davies nodded. He didn't agree with the policy, but people were upset about the buzz regarding aliens abducting an airplane. If Darrell Gwinner hadn't been on that plane, no one would have thought twice about it. As far as Mr. Davies was concerned, it was good riddance. His daughter, Kristin, had been acting secretive ever since she took the job as Darrell's assistant at the Exchange. He had a feeling something shady was going on.

"Okay. And you said?" Mr. Davies asked.

"I asked if she meant space aliens or illegal aliens. Then Mrs. Tomlinson sent me here and said we'd have no mention of undocumented visitors in her classroom." Johnny stopped. As far as he was concerned, that was the end of the discussion.

Mr. Davies sighed. It was another school policy he didn't agree with and most teachers didn't pay attention to.

"Liberal do-gooders gone amuck," he said. "Do you have a costume ready?"

"Yes, sir," Johnny said, opening his sketchbook. He showed Mr. Davies the pictures he'd drawn of aliens and how his costume would look. Mr. Davies especially liked the flippers.

"Okay, Johnny. I'm going to suspend you for one day. Tomorrow. Today's almost over. That means you don't have to come to school tomorrow, so you can dress in any goddam costume you want to. I hope you have some fun."

"Yes, sir. Um… Am I supposed to be upset or happy?"

"Well, you should look upset when you see your school friends, but you don't have to *be* upset. Let's keep this between you and me. I don't think I need to call your parents," Mr. Davies said with a wink.

Johnny grinned at him and sat quietly in the outer office drawing in his notebook until the end of school bell rang.

"Don't you want to get a bag of candy for the trick-or-treaters?" Josephine asked at the Dollar General.

Oswald frowned at her. He'd spent most of the afternoon with Stacy. In Stacy as much as possible. There might even have been an accident or two, but she was married, so it didn't make a difference if she got pregnant again. That girl was as tight as she'd been when she'd entered high school and he'd entered her the first time. But the idea of passing out candy to children on Halloween was the worst idea Oswald could think of. He didn't say anything about that.

"It's all too expensive," he said. "I'll buy a few bags of it next weekend when it's all on sale."

It might have sounded like he would give it away then, but it would go into his storehouse and keep him in candy for the next few months. At least until the Christmas candy went on sale.

Josephine continued to attempt being flirtatious with him, but she was almost as old as he was, for Christ's sake. *What was she doing flirting?*

As he dragged his cart home, he encountered little Johnny Malone, skipping happily along the sidewalk. The two almost collided.

"Watch where you're going!" Oswald shouted, reaching for his Ruger before remembering he'd left it with Stacy.

"Sorry, sir!" Johnny gulped. Having Mrs. Tomlinson mad at him was nothing compared to having Mr. Kennedy mad.

"What are you so happy about?" Oswald growled.

"Oh… um… well… I kind of got suspended from school for a day," Johnny said. "That means I can go around in my Halloween costume all day tomorrow. It will be so cool! Are you going to shoot trick-or-treaters this year?"

"Yeah. I won't kill any of them. I'll use rubber bullets. Crowd control rounds. You come around the compound and I'll put one right in your skinny ass!"

"Oh, wow! Not me. If you want to shoot a really skinny ass, you should try Becca's. I don't think she's got an ass at all! Besides," Johnny lowered his voice. "I heard she plans to try TPing your wall again this year."

"Hmm. Some kids never learn. Well, watch out for aliens," Oswald said, pulling his cart past Johnny.

Johnny breathed a sigh of relief.

"I've got it all arranged," Brett said as he pressed himself against Bridget. He'd driven the truck to school, just so he could drive Bridget home with a little detour down the track behind the corn maze. He'd been working all week laying out the maze according to the map he'd drawn. People could get lost in it. It excited him.

"Take it easy. We aren't going all the way in this pickup," she said, pushing his hand away from her crotch. She didn't mind the hand on her breast. She was used to that.

"Of course not. But tomorrow night, I'll drive the tractor around to pick up all the kids we invited. I'm going to put fresh straw down on the trailer—not that scratchy hay we had last year. We'll go out and howl at the moon for a while and then I'll drive back and let all the others off in town. All except you. We'll head back to the farm and park in the barn, then we've got the rest of the night on a nice straw bed where no one can see us."

"How am I supposed to stay out all night? You know I have a midnight curfew," Bridget said, letting him push her bra up so he could handle her bare breast.

"That's the brilliant part of the plan. Sheldon and Elaine are going to hide in the straw when I let the other kids off. They're staying with us for the night. You tell your parents you're staying with Elaine and she'll tell hers she's staying with you. No one the wiser. Sheldon is telling his parents that he's staying the night with me so he can help with picking the rest of this corn Saturday."

"You mean you want to do it with Sheldon and Elaine right there to see us?" Bridget asked in shock.

"They're going to be too busy with each other to see anything we're doing."

"Sheldon and Elaine. Wow! I never guessed."

Bridget got lost kissing Brett and guessed she didn't mind his hand worming its way between her legs after all.

4
New Capital

MEANWHILE, SOMEWHERE OVER THE rainbow, Darrell and Janelle were helping the aliens plan their invasion.

"We'll land this at the airport in Washington, DC. Everyone will come out to greet us and we'll just announce the takeover on TV. People won't even know we're aliens until after the announcement. We'll all copy the bodies of the people on the plane. In a few weeks, we'll start dropping these guys and the others we've taken over the past hundred years in random places all over the country. People will assume they're just aliens, too." Haro said.

"Hmm. I might have a better idea," Darrell said. "Washington, DC is a cesspit and it's way too far from most of the country for people to care if it's been invaded. It's irrelevant. We could do it with fewer invaders and make people believe we're all over the country."

"I do like the way you say *we*," Zeta said, stroking Darrell's always hard cock. She found Janelle's hand there at the same time and grinned at the humans.

"Fill us in on your idea," Haro said.

"My hometown is smack dab in the middle of the country. Easy to reach for anyone. Plus, it's small. If we take over a small town in the Midwest, people will automatically think we've got troops in every part of the country. Land a plane full of people in Washington—or better yet, a flying saucer—and people there will panic and go crazy.

"The president will be launched into the air in Air Force One. Watch for that and bring him onboard. No one will know he disappeared because he'll be out of radar contact anyway as a safety protocol. If you can copy bodies, copy his, too. Then when we land, you can announce that there was an invasion of Washington and members of congress may actually be aliens. They'll be too confused suspecting each other to do anything. Announce that you've moved the capital to Longview, Kansas during this time of emergency so you can more easily respond to needs nationwide. Oh, and mention that you negotiated with the aliens for the release of these passengers who you have subsequently appointed to the cabinet, senate, and congress."

"What about the Supreme Court?" Haro asked as he pulled Janelle onto his lap and began growing his erection into her.

"Everybody already thinks they're aliens," Darrell said.

"I'll run it by high command as soon as I finish this mating. I mean meeting. Oh, baby, you're good!" Haro moaned.

"Do me more!" Janelle cried out. "Let me suck on one of your tentacles. Yes! Oh, God, yes!"

THEY WORKED ON the timing of events, what the aliens who land in DC should look like, when to snatch the president's plane, and when to make their landing in Kansas. This was going to be a great day. They'd covertly land a few aliens in Longview early dressed up in Halloween costumes so they could have a welcoming committee in place. It was Halloween, after all. Everyone would expect crazy clowns, witches, hobos, and sexy bare-butt nuns. Longview called itself the Halloween capital of the world. Everyone dressed up for this holiday. People came from all over to parade around town in their costumes and go to the haunted church.

Everyone except the Evangelicals and Pentecostals. Everybody figured they were already in costume anyway.

There was an issue of where to stay, even though the aliens didn't really have a regular sleep clock.

"There's a suitable place for the president," Darrell said. "One guy in town has an eight-foot wall around his compound. It's well-stocked with food and weapons. Um… That latter could be a problem. He's a gun freak and is always armed."

"We have excellent negotiators," Zeta said. "We'll get him to give up his compound without a shot being fired. Or with a shot. Whichever works."

It was decided that Darrell and Janelle would play themselves in the charade. Darrell fully intended to take Janelle home with him and just tell Stacy that she was part of a harem now. He figured he'd bring Kristin with him. That would give Stacy some help with the little tyke. She'd be okay with that.

The supreme commander approved the invasion plan and congratulated Haro and the rest of the planning team on the unusual battle plan. By the time the full invasion force arrived the next day, the country would be mostly pacified. The 'president' would order the armed forces to stand down because we were allies visiting to strengthen the country's position in the world.

They estimated fifty-five to sixty percent of the adult population of the US would believe the whole thing was fake news and go about their day as previously planned. Thirty-five to forty percent would believe the president was a fucking genius who had negotiated with space aliens and made the country twice as powerful as it had ever been. The other five percent would believe the story of the aliens and would attempt to fight them off. The aliens considered that an acceptable amount of collateral damage.

"Zeta, I have concerning news," an alien said, coming into the situation room.

Zeta and Haro were two of the principal officers of the aliens, so it wasn't unusual for people to rush in with reports. They were the ones in charge of abductions for the past several decades.

"What is it, Dola?" Zeta asked.

"It's about your daughter."

Everyone froze. The two humans had never heard that Zeta had a daughter. She inhaled deeply and her human form fell away from the tentacled alien.

"Speak!" Zeta said.

"She was to have been dropped at the target in the second wave. Orin is a fairly new saucer driver and miscalculated the landing zone. He came in low over Texas and some cowboys started shooting at the saucer. He bounced into the desert and many of the landing party members were thrown from the saucer."

"Have they been captured?" Haro asked in alarm.

"No. The damage was superficial and Orin got the saucer back in the air. He thought he had all the passengers, but when they landed in Kansas and disembarked, Ohna was not on board. Orin cautiously scouted the area where they'd landed, but could find no sign of her," Dola concluded her report.

She stood aside, possibly fearing what Zeta's reaction would be. Gradually, Zeta's human form returned to her. Everyone breathed a sigh of relief.

"After we've completed the mission tomorrow, we'll mount a search," Zeta said. "Ohna knows and understands her earth survival skills. She may be in hiding and we'll find her. If she's been captured, there will be reports once we land. Something tells me, though, that Ohna is still in transit. She might make it to Longview before we do."

"Let's assess any damage we have to the landing saucer and make sure Orin gets some remedial flight training," Haro said.

Everyone went back to work.

OHN'A. MAYBE IF she'd crashed in Hawai'i people could pronounce it. In Texas, she'd be thankful if they just said Oh No.

She was lucky she got thrown out of the saucer where she did. It was remote and there were no people in view. She'd bounced all the way across a ridge and before she could get back to the saucer, Orin had everyone back in and had taken off again. *See if he ever gets laid again.* At least not by her!

She needed to get a move on. The folks who shot at the saucer would all be mounted in their pickup trucks and racing to where they thought it had crashed. Ohna wanted to be miles away before they got there. It looked like Texas. She'd studied American geography, and knew Kansas was north. She headed that direction, discarding the wooden shoes and little Dutch pinafore that was supposed to be her costume when they landed in Longview. She morphed into her tentacled alien form. It moved a lot faster than the human form.

If her assumption was correct and she was in Texas, it was four or five hundred miles to Longview, Kansas. She was going to need transportation. Preferably something that came with a driver. She needed to practice a little before she just jumped behind a wheel and took off.

She'd run north for a few miles when she finally saw a house ahead. A bang rang out from the house while Ohna was still some distance away. She saw a white pickup raise a cloud of dust as it tore away from the little house and up a dirt road.

Perfectly good transportation just too far away for her to catch it. Ohna hurried to the house and looked in.

A naked woman was lying on the floor of the living room, bleeding from her chest.

The aliens were all indoctrinated before they started this invasion. They weren't to harm anyone if it could be helped. They all knew that anyone who was injured during this period would blame it on the aliens. Didn't seem fair, but it was the human way. Ohna just knew she needed to help the bleeding woman.

Fortunately, over the past fifty years, she'd learned a fair amount about human physiology and medicine. Primitive stuff. She shifted back into her human shape and rushed inside. She had her own first aid kit in a pouch of her hip. Not on her hip. In her hip.

The wounded woman was in bad shape, but Ohna was able to extract the bullet and close the wound. The way the woman stared at her, she wondered if her tentacles were showing.

"You should heal up fine now," Ohna said. "Okay?"

"Who are you and how'd you get here?"

"I was kind of hiking," Ohna said. "I heard the shot and came running."

"How can I thank you? I thought I'd die right here on the floor. And why were you hiking naked?"

"Yeah. I sort of lost my costume and could use some different clothes. Got anything I could borrow?"

"Sure. I don't know if they'll fit, though. We're a little different," the woman said.

"I can fix that," Ohna said. "I'm Ohna. I'm from outer space and I need to meet my family in Longview, Kansas."

"Outer space? Are you one of the aliens the president was posting about? Are you going to eat us all?"

"Oh, no! We don't eat people. We're trying to save the world. What's your name?"

Ohna remembered to close up her hip pouch.

"I'm Cecelia Warden."

Cecelia wasn't sure why she was so comfortable being naked in front of this naked alien stranger, but she'd been taking her clothes off at the BlaQ Diamond since she was eighteen. It seemed natural. Besides, this Ohna was really sexy. Right in front of Cecelia's eyes, Ohna started to morph into her perfect double.

"Oh, hell, yes!" Cecelia cried. "I wondered what it was about me that gave guys a hard-on! I'd fuck you if I had a dick!"

"Later," Ohna said. "Could you get us both some clothes? I don't think it will be safe for you to stay out here alone. That shooter might come back to finish the job."

"Damn Bobby Bill. Followed me out here and then wouldn't pay for the privilege. Can I come to Longview with you? We can be twins!" Cecelia said.

"Sure, honey. We just need to get moving pretty quickly."

Ohna had even copied Cecelia's Texas accent. Cecelia opened a closet and pointed.

"Whatever you want!"

"Yeah. Like I said. Later," Ohna sighed. She empathized with Cecelia's interest in fucking her. She'd mount the girl in a second if she had a second to spare.

The humans she'd looked at when selecting one for her body were all in cold storage. Ohna had never actually been in the presence of and interacting with a real naked human woman before. She could feel a lot of twitching going on in her genitals.

"I hate to cover any of that up, but if we have to travel all the way across Oklahoma, we'd better put regular clothes on," Cecelia said.

She handed a pair of jeans and a plaid shirt to Ohna, then chose an almost identical outfit for herself. She never bothered with underwear or a bra, so didn't offer one to Ohna. She was a perfect match for Cecelia, right down to her shaved pussy. Even the boots fit her. Cecelia handed her a hat and grabbed her purse.

"You don't have any ID, do you?" Cecelia asked.

"No. I'm a real live undocumented alien."

"We'll have to share mine. And you can call me Cece. We'll take my car."

They headed out the back door and Cece led Ohna to a garage containing a bright yellow Mustang. The car threw a cloud of dust behind it as they headed toward the freeway.

THURSDAY NIGHT, STACY had just finished helping Willis Davies unload a burden he'd been carrying in his balls all day. Of course, he gave her a nice cash gift before he left but really, Stacy screwed him just because he was Kristin's father and the elementary school principal. She kept a close eye on that little bitch. Darrell wasn't the only one fucking that little eighteen-year-old cunt. Stacy liked the taste of pussy, too.

She had just stepped out of a refreshing shower and was wrapped in a towel when she heard a knock on her door. Without bothering to dress, she ran downstairs in her towel to see who was there at ten o'clock at night. If it was another guy who just wanted to help her a little, she wouldn't need clothes anyway. She'd have to tell him that he should come to the back door if he wanted something like that.

She was surprised to find Bert Beeson, the town mayor, at her front door.

"Mr. Mayor. Uh… How can I help you?" she asked, clutching at the towel.

"Stacy, I have something you need to see," he said officiously.

Most guys just *sent* her dick pics. She didn't have to look at them live. Oh, well.

"Come in. Please excuse the way I'm dressed. Or not dressed. Just got out of the shower, you know."

"How you dress or don't dress in your own home is your business," he said, pulling out his phone.

He came here to show me his dick pic in person?

"Please don't ask how I happened upon this. Let's just say, I'm acquainted with Janelle Cummbridge," Bert said.

"Janelle Cummbridge?" Stacy asked. "Sounds like a porn star."

"Well… yes. She has an Only Fans page. Her site went dark Tuesday evening when she was expected to be online doing a performance. Fans have been getting concerned, but this evening, she posted a cryptic message that said, 'On DCA1427.' I'm sure you know that flight number. It's the plane your husband was on that went missing."

"And the post went up tonight?" Stacy asked. "Does that mean they're all alive somewhere?"

"We don't know. I checked the passenger list and, of course, Janelle Cummbridge is just a stage name and it wasn't listed on the airline's list of passengers that was released this afternoon. She could have sent this before the plane crashed, or whatever it did, and just set it to post on Thursday. Performers often pre-record and set their post for a certain day and time of release," Bert said.

"You know a lot about this stuff," Stacy grinned at him. Her towel seemed to be coming loose.

"As mayor of this fine town, I need to keep up with what is happening that might affect our fine citizens," Bert sniffed. "But I thought you should see this."

He handed his phone to Stacy and pressed the play button.

"I'm here with my new friend DG. We're getting to know each other really well. Say something DG."

"I found something here that will make this flight worthwhile!"

Darrell had his arm around the girl in the next seat and gave her a squeeze.

"That no good lying cheating son of a bitch!" Stacy said. "Where are they?"

"It's obvious the recording has been edited and it ends abruptly. Um… Right after they had sex in the toilet. I don't know if it was before the plane disappeared or if it was sent from someplace afterward. I'm sorry, Stacy."

Stacy jumped up from the sofa where she'd been sitting next to Bert to watch the video. Her movement was so fast that she left the towel on the sofa. All Bert could do was stare at the nineteen-year-old.

"I'll kill him! I'll kill her! I'll kill myself!" she said, stomping around her living room.

Bert had the presence of mind to switch to record on his phone. He thought he was being sneaky, but Stacy was all over him.

"Great idea! We'll record a little vengeance for my dear husband," Stacy said, approaching Bert and straddling him, right above his phone. This was better than anything he'd seen on OF. "Let's get that big boner out of your pants, honey. Keep recording as you slide it right into my bare pussy. No, don't worry about a condom. If I get pregnant, Good Times Darrell will just have to raise it knowing it's my vengeance baby. God, yes! Why have you been hiding this big boy? Why are you single? I know a dozen girls who would kill to have a beast like this in their pussy. Yeah! Pump it in and out. I'm going to make you cum in a flood. And you just keep recording as my pussy lets your cum run out of me. Sorry, Miss Cummbridge. You got the short end of the dick, so to speak. Yes! Cum in me!"

Bert was obedient and flooded her pussy. He kept recording as she lifted off him and his semen began to run out of her.

"Now send me both of those vids," Stacy commanded, grabbing her towel. "And get out of here. I don't do guys for free, but that vid is payment enough."

Bert sent her the two videos and then stuffed his cock back in his pants. He almost ran to the door and out into the night. He'd be playing that one over and over tonight.

No matter how exciting the day had been for people in the town, it was only Thursday night. They had to go to work and to school the next day. Even BJ's Roadhouse out on the highway out of town was empty early as people headed home to sleep. When it came right down to it, Longview was just a sleepy little Midwestern town, but Friday would be a big day. It was Halloween!

So, no one was awake when a saucer landed at midnight out in the very cornfield where Brett had worked with his buddy Sheldon to create a corn maze. It came in with no lights, but it was hot enough on entry to glow a little and singe a circle in the middle of the maze. That would raise Brett's eyebrows!

A hundred aliens disembarked from the saucer, each wearing the identity of one of the thousands of people they'd abducted over the past couple of centuries. The originals were in cold storage up in space and would be dropped off in different parts of the world after the invasion was completed.

Until then, thousands of aliens were up there trying on different looks as if they were in Abercrombie and Fitch. There was a lot of alien laughter as they commented on each other's looks and whether anyone would be able to tell they weren't human. Darrell and Janelle walked through the changing rooms, criticizing some looks and praising others. Wherever they went the aliens wanted their opinion of the body they'd put on. They were quite the celebrities.

Zeta, Haro, and the rest of the DCA1427 flight crew, of course, already had bodies they were comfortable with. They'd been making trips into the US for a century or more. But Janelle helped them select clothes to take with them so they didn't always have to wear their flight uniforms.

Clothing was one of the biggest issues. Over half of the costumes that had been prepared were at least fifty years out of date. Some had been copied from other countries that had completely different styles. Most of these could be used for Halloween costumes, but for daily wear, they were far out of date.

Makeup was applied, masks tried on, and hundreds of Halloween costumes were prepared. Each alien had a small bag with a change of clothes, and when they were costumed and presentable, they boarded the shuttle saucer and were dropped off near where they would need to be in the morning.

In Longview, the hundred aliens in the advance deployment were all dressed in Halloween costumes that concealed the identity of the wearer. It wasn't so much that they were afraid someone would recognize them. Longview was a community of a little over 3,750 souls, and people were familiar enough with each other that having strangers walking around in town would be a serious risk that someone would stop them and ask them who they were.

They all had a cookie cutter story about passing through or hearing Longview was the center of the country and had a great Halloween celebration. If a person heard enough of the stories, he'd recognize that they were all essentially the same.

There was a selection of scary clowns who had a backstory of having been on set for a new horror film and thought they'd visit nearby Longview for the Halloween festival. A number of animal costumes were explained as being people attending a furry convention in Salina who had decided to attend the festivities in Longview. Thirteen 'men and women' in traditional Dutch costumes complete with wooden shoes said they had been at a family heritage reunion some twenty miles away and heard Longview was the place to celebrate Halloween. There were eighteen different themes, but they all had a similar back-story. It was the best Darrell and Janelle could come up with.

The aliens who were dropped in more densely populated areas didn't worry so much about Halloween backstories or costumes. It was far less likely that they would be identified as a stranger when the place had a few million people who were all strangers to each other. Copying a hundred-year-old specimen was no problem, as long as he or she was dressed in contemporary clothing.

Saucer after saucer full of aliens were dropped without incident overnight. No one was the wiser.

5
Flight 19

"**I** MIGHT HAVE THOUGHT OF a problem," Darrell said sheepishly, calling Zeta and Haro aside. Their passengers would be among the last to embark since they'd be traveling by plane.

"What is it?" Haro asked, concerned.

"Well, this is a jumbo jet. It takes about three miles of runway to land it. The runway in Longview is about half a mile. Not only that, it isn't paved. It's just a dirt strip," Darrell explained. They might all have to land by saucer instead of using the planes.

Haro breathed an alien sigh of relief.

"Is that all? We knew that. Neither DCA1427 nor Air Force One will be flying under their own power. The tractor beam will catch us and set us down with only enough noise and taxiing to call attention to our arrival. We've even arranged to have steps delivered to the little strip or no one would be able to get out of the plane."

"Thank goodness. You guys think of everything."

"Well, you and Janelle and Zeta and I have been on the overall strategy for taking things over. We've had several teams dealing with the tactics. We had you working on costumes and the landing site cover because you know the area

"

and the fashions. We have an entire team who are in charge of neutralizing the armed forces. It wouldn't do to have a B-52 Stratofortress dropping bombs on us."

"We have B-52s inside the US?" Darrell asked.

"Don't worry. We'll have an aide stationed beside you to whisper appropriate responses to you whenever you might need to speak in your new role."

"Not to seem too ignorant, but what is my new role?" Darrell asked.

"Oh! We didn't consider it too important for now, but you'll be the president's new Secretary of State. Remember, we've been studying your people for a long time," Haro said.

"What's my role?" Janelle asked.

"We'll re-establish the Department of Education," Zeta said. "You are to be the new Secretary of Sex Education. That's the only part of human education we consider to be all that important. We'll be replacing what's left of the top-level scientists with our own people. It really won't be important to have people educated in the kind of primitive sciences your people have been studying so slowly for so many years. Things like math can be taught in sex education far more effectively than in an arithmetic class."

"I've always thought that!" Janelle exclaimed. "I can't wait to demonstrate the techniques and pleasures of alien sex."

"I hope you'll save a little of that for me," Darrell said, patting Janelle's bottom.

"Have you been lacking anything since we got here?" she giggled.

"Not at all."

"I can't wait to educate your wife and secretary on the ways three women can please a man," Janelle said. "And an alien or two," she added, giving Zeta a heartfelt kiss.

It was less than two hours from Wichita Falls to Oklahoma City. Considerably less, the way Cece drove. They pulled into a Love's Travel Stop just before I-44 and I-35 split headed north. Cece put almost fifteen gallons into the little Mustang. She apologized for not having had her car gassed up and ready to roll before they left her house.

"There will be a day soon when you won't need gas for your car," Ohna said brightly. "Over the past few decades, we engineered a system that uses water for power. Tried to get it introduced here, but people have been stubborn. Especially down South here. Good ol' boys like their oil."

"Speaking of a good ol' boy, take a look yonder at that fine specimen of manhood," Cece drawled.

She directed Ohna's gaze to a young stud standing near the store entrance. He was fit and wearing a jeans jacket over a muscle shirt that was tight enough to show his abs. He wore tight jeans and cowboy boots.

"Wow!" Ohna said. She'd spent enough time studying earth to appreciate the human male form.

"He's not one of yours, is he?" Cece asked.

"No. The guys on the ship would be fighting over a body like that," Ohna said.

"Then let's make him ours," Cece suggested.

Ohna copied Cece's hip swing as they headed to the door of the store. On her way past, Cece paused long enough to lightly stroke the boy's cheek with her finger and wink at him. Ohna followed suit. She knew there were a lot of mating rituals humans went through and Cece seemed to have them all perfected. The boy pushed away from the wall and followed them inside, carrying his small backpack.

After the girls emerged from the bathroom, they found the boy loitering near the snack food.

"You hungry, cowboy?" Cece asked. She and Ohna had unbuttoned a couple of buttons of their shirts and tied the tails beneath their boobs. The boy looked at her longingly.

"Starving," he said.

"Let's see if we can get you filled up. Maybe later you can fill us up. Headed north?"

"Wherever," he said.

She had him select a bunch of food. The two women selected some snacks as well. Ohna watched Cece and simply duplicated her selection of snacks. As soon as they got outside the store, the boy started wolfing down the hotdog he'd grabbed. They walked toward the car.

"What's your name, cowboy?" Cece asked.

"Austin."

"Austin what?"

"Just Austin. Might have had another name once, but I don't remember it."

"No ID, right?"

"Yeah."

"Well, Austin, I'm Cece and this is Ohna. We're the Warden twins. You just became our brother, Austin Warden. If the po-po or Gestapo decide we're of interest, the story is I just picked up you two to make a fast trip to Kansas because our grandma is dying. You two didn't have any time to pick up your purse or wallet. Got it?"

Both Ohna and Austin nodded. Ohna and Cece had come up with the story during the first part of the trip, while they were still a good three hours from Longview.

"So, tell us about our brother Austin," Ohna said.

"Don't remember my parents, either. I got passed around from foster home to foster home until I got sick of it and just walked away. Been living on my own ever since," Austin said.

"Where?" Ohna asked.

"Oh, here and there. I found an abandoned trailer in a storage area and stayed there until they came and tore it down this fall. Then I thought I'd better move. Don't know why I chose to go north. Thought Dallas would be a good place, but they aren't kind to vagrants or street people. And ICE just started rounding up everyone they didn't like the looks of. Saw a buddy of mine hauled away by guys in masks. Never saw him again," Austin said.

"All right, now look," Cece broke in. "There's a .45 and three clips in the glove box. I'll stop for local or state cops, but anyone shows up in a mask and tries to stop us, Ohna, you get out that gun and hand it to me. As far as I'm concerned, masked men are robbers and rapists. We shoot them down rather than surrender."

Ohna looked in the glove box and saw the gun and shells.

"We won't need to worry about that in Longview. Enough of my people are there that they'll respond immediately to a threat," she said.

"How'd your people get to Longview?"

"Got dropped off in the night. Probably still getting a shuttle or two. It ain't quite daylight yet. They all got warned that even at Halloween, people in that kind of mask would get shot."

"You two sound like sisters," Austin laughed. "And you both look good enough to eat."

"Think I might give you a chance at that," Cece said. "Ohna, have you figured out how to drive this hotrod?"

"I think I can manage it now."

"Point it down the highway and press the accelerator. If you happen to get stopped, just show my license. You'll be me and I'll be you."

Cece pulled off the highway to switch with Ohna. It was going to be tight in the backseat of the Mustang, but Cece was determined. They pushed the front passenger seat forward as far as it would go and started immediately removing each other's clothes. Ohna adjusted the mirror so she could watch.

"WE'RE BEGINNING TO get reports from our agents in Washington, New York, and Florida," Haro announced to his team. "It's almost sunrise and people are beginning to head for work and for school. Of course, it will be two hours yet before the government and financial offices open. We have agents among the laborers, keeping watch over the city waking up and a timeline for starting things in DC."

"That's great. There isn't much of anything in the government or financial world that's worth anything once you've taken over," Darrell said.

"Well, we won't be just randomly shooting people down," Haro said. Janelle had just perched herself on his lap and was being filled by his ever-growing appendage. "On the other hand, we won't be stopping people from shooting each other. I'm afraid we'll be in for a few bloody days. That's why your instruction is going to be so important, Madam Secretary. We want people converted over to the old 'make love, not war' mindset as quickly as possible."

"Shoot into me, Haro. I love the feeling of your sex tentacle in my pussy."

"Have I let you feel this before?" Haro asked. He began twirling his appendage inside her vagina.

"Oh, God! I feel like I've got an egg beater in my cunt! Only it's not sharp. It's like a little tornado that's twirling around and touching all my… Oh… shit… yes!"

Janelle was one happy Secretary of Sex Education. She'd been recording everything since she boarded DCA1427. They'd allowed her to post the edited version of her first encounter with Darrell, assuming no one would know who they were or where they were. Once the takeover was accomplished, she'd be able to start posting the sex videos with Haro and Zeta, too.

"Mr. President, we have a situation," the secret service agent said, waking the president.

George Constantis was specially selected for this position. He was the only one who could wake the president from sleep without being fired on the spot. No one knew that the former agent known as George Constantis was in cold storage up in space. The alien in his place had fully adopted the former agent's look and personality.

"I'm not in the mood for an interruption," the president said. "I was just about to enter a dressing room filled with naked teenagers."

"That's a memory, sir. Not a dream. You can relive it any time," George said.

"All right. So, what's the big deal?"

The president bounced a couple of times before managing to get his bulk to sit up in the bed. George handed him clothes as he described the situation.

"A squadron of Navy fighters has just landed at Andrews," George said.

"Is that a problem? It's a joint base," the president growled.

"It's Flight 19, sir. They've been missing for eighty years."

"That's before I was born! Go check again. It can't be the same flight," the president said.

He reached for his phone and began typing a message on his social media account.

"Halloween prank! Navy fighter pilots pretend to be pilots missing for eighty years. HaHa!"

"Sir, they claim to be the same pilots who lost compass functionality on December 5, 1945 in the Bermuda Triangle," George said. "The fourteen crewmen all appear to be in their twenties."

"Any explanations?" the president asked.

"They claim they were caught in a time warp and were given a special assignment as they were transported to this time. The message included the coordinates and directions to Andrews, and the instruction to 'protect the president.' We believe you should be ready to go to Air Force One," George said.

"I knew it. I knew you were coming," the president muttered. "Covfefe. The aliens have invaded."

"What, sir?"

"The Covfefe. I met them years ago. We should have grabbed the rest of the Democrats in congress. They're all illegal aliens. Call the generals to the Oval Office! Stat!"

"Yes, Doctor," George chuckled.

NONETHELESS, IN THIRTY minutes, the president arrived in the Oval Office where the Joint Chiefs of Staff and the Secretary of the War Department were waiting. None of them looked as sharp as the president in his blue suit and red tie. His hair was perfectly coifed and sprayed stiff. Fresh spray tan had been applied to his face.

"We have confirmation that the Navy fighters that landed at Andrews are, indeed, Flight 19," Admiral O'Connor reported.

"The serial numbers of the aircraft and the blood samples from the crew all match."

"Yeah, yeah. Satisfy yourselves. Just keep them at the ready," the president said. "We have a critical emergency."

The Joint Chiefs seemed to wonder what kind of emergency trumped the arrival of a flight that had been missing for eighty years.

"We have not been effective enough in rounding up illegal aliens!" the president shouted. "Congress has been infiltrated. All the women in congress and the senate are suspect. And all the rest of the Democrats. And Senator Cannon—thinks he can vote against me! Double the number of National Guard in DC. No, triple it. Head to the Capitol and arrest them all. If anyone resists, shoot them. And send a company to arrest the judges of the Supreme Court. Any other judges that try to get in our way. I'm declaring a National Emergency. We need to be ready to fight for our great country! Go!"

There was no discussion allowed. That wasn't unusual. They were used to following absurd orders from the president. Besides, four of the five leaders called in by the president were replicas of the original chiefs. The Secretary of War had been an alien plant all the way back in his television days.

Of course, bringing several hundred more troops into the capital wasn't unnoticed. There were only a few restaurants still open in the nation's capital. Hotels were nearly empty. People avoided the troops like they avoided the police.

Soon the rumors of aliens having taken over congress were louder than the squeaky tracks of the tanks that slowly surrounded the Capitol. Several members of the house and senate heard the rumors and turned their drivers west. They intended to hide out in the mountains of West Virginia and Pennsylvania.

Others paused to arm themselves before heading into town.

Armed locals suddenly hit the streets. It was only a matter of time before violence erupted.

"My fellow citizens of this great country. I want you to know there is no country greater than this one. We are the focus and envy of the world. And, it turns out, of other worlds, too," the president said in his hastily called address to the nation.

"For a few days, you've been hearing alarming news about a pending invasion from outer space. We're meeting this attack head-on. I've mobilized the United States Army, Navy, Air Force, Coast Guard, Marines, National Guard, and Reserves—brave *men*, all of them. Probably no military force in the world that is as competent as our force and I've mobilized them to protect Americans all over the country. They aren't going to let any rumors of aliens touch our great citizens.

"If you aren't a citizen, I'm sorry for you, but we offered you a way out and you refused to go. The rapists and murderers and drug dealers who flooded into our country across the previous administration's open borders are on their own now. That was a terrible administration. Worst president ever. Stole the election. Now, we have enemies at hand and are going to devote our energy to protecting our brave businessmen who make our country so rich that everyone else wants what we have.

"It doesn't make a difference if they are disguised as judges or senators or other Democrats. This isn't a democracy—it's a republic. We don't want any more reference to democrocritics. So, I want to tell you to protect yourselves and join our great military in fighting off this threat.

"I am going to meet this head on and negotiate with the aliens myself. I'll end this invasion in time for dinner. I should get a Nobel Peace Prize for this. No one else is going to go face the aliens. I'm the great Peace President. It's very unfair that they haven't recognized this already."

The president abruptly left the press room and went directly to the concrete garden to board a helicopter to Andrews where Air Force One and Flight 19 awaited his arrival. No one understood anything he said.

"Mr. President, should we awaken the first lady and your son?" asked an aide as they left by the side entrance.

"Don't bother. They'll be fine," he said, crawling up into the helicopter.

BY THE TIME the president reached Andrews, shots were being fired near the capitol. To no one's particular surprise, shots were being exchanged in the House Chamber. There weren't many in the large room due to the shutdown, but they could hear shots elsewhere in the building as well.

"This is why you wanted the government shut down! You prepared this all for the aliens!" someone on the left shouted at his colleague on the right.

"Now we know why you wanted us all disarmed! You wanted it easier for the aliens to take control!" a voice from the righthand side of the chamber shouted as he came up shooting. He was surprised when a volley was returned.

"Do you think just because we want better gun laws that we're unarmed?" shouted an opponent. "Take that, you child-raping sack of shit!"

It seemed as though a civil war had broken out in the chamber. And as desperate aides and lower employees burst out the doors of the Capitol, they were immediately swept up by soldiers in riot gear and masks.

The battles were not confined to the House and Senate

Chambers. Beyond the Capitol, there was also gunfire in the halls of the Supreme Court. It was mostly lawyers shooting at each other, so no one was terribly concerned. The justices hadn't arrived at the Supreme Court Building. In fact, no one was sure where they were. No one had heard from the eleven old men and women.

The battles spread throughout the nation's capital. Self-proclaimed militias took up stations at random locations, declaring they were protecting the Treasury, the National Air and Space Museum, the Lincoln Memorial, and Starbucks. No one really understood the logic of their deployment, but if they crossed paths, they exchanged fire.

HARLAN GRAVES AND Millie MacDonald heard the news in the morning and jumped into Harlan's Bronco with the scratched sides to head toward West Virginia. They hadn't bothered to dress when they got out of bed, but grabbed bathrobes and slippers as they rushed out the door.

"Where are we going, Harlan?"

"Right to the heart of it, Millie," he said. "There's a back-woods ho out there who knows exactly what's happening. We're throwing our lot in with her."

Millie turned in her seat and examined the gun cases attached to their seatbacks.

"I hope you bought some ammo for these babies," she said.

Harlan glanced over at her. Millie's robe gaped open as she examined the guns and he definitely saw the babies he had ammo for. He reached over and squeezed her left tit. Millie swatted at his hand and then opened her robe wide.

Harlan nearly drove off the road.

6
Covfefe

"YO! WE MADE IT, sista!" Cece called from the front seat. "Where should I go?"

Ohna groaned. Austin finally let go of a powerful stream into her cunt. She and Cece had switched places again near Wichita, Kansas and Ohna had only managed a little more than an hour with Austin's meat in her. He was amazed that he'd had anything to give her after Cece had milked him for close to two hours, but Ohna had kept him up with incredibly sensual movements in her pussy that had brought out this spray of more than he thought his body could produce.

"What time is it, baby?" Ohna asked. Austin struggled to look at a non-existent watch.

"Six-thirty," Cece responded.

"There's a little place called Sarah Lee's Diner on Second Street at Kansas Street. It opens at six for locals to fuel up. That's where we'll meet up with my friends at seven," Ohna said.

"You mean people get up at six?" Cece exclaimed. "I've never seen the dawn from that side. Usually if I'm up at six, I haven't been to bed yet. Or at least to sleep."

She was feeling incredibly lively for all she'd been through the previous night. She'd had that nasty Bobby Bill follow her to her house and fuck her, then get mad when she demanded he pay her and he shot her. Then an undocumented immigrant showed up at the house and healed her, then copied her look so perfectly she wanted to fuck her. They'd driven up to Oklahoma City where they picked up Austin and half an hour later, she'd been folded nearly in half while he fucked her in the back seat. She'd taken over driving again while Ohna did the same thing in the back seat. And Austin looked like he was ready to go at it again!

As good as she felt, though, it would be even better if this Sarah Lee had decent coffee.

She spotted a coin-op car wash and pulled the Mustang in there before heading downtown to the diner.

"Kitty needs a quick wash before we head to the diner," Cece said. "Get the road dust out of her."

They piled out of the car and saw Cece stripping. They'd misunderstood 'Kitty' to be what she called the car. Ohna and Austin stripped, too. Cece did spray down the car to get three states' worth of dust off it, but then they took turns spraying each other down and cleaning the kitties.

It was great fun, but they had to get to the diner. They used a roll of paper towel Cece had in the back of the Mustang to dry themselves off, then got dressed again. Looking like a bunch of fresh Texas kids, they headed for the diner.

It seemed like a lot of people were headed that direction. Sarah Lee's was a popular place in the morning. Everyone in the diner was wearing a costume of some kind—often with a mask. Longview went all out for Halloween. From somewhere, Ohna produced a bonnet with a stylized red cross on it. It had points at the ends of each of the arms.

"What's that for? I thought we were just dressing up as ourselves," Austin asked.

"Yeah, mostly. I have to have a way for my people to recognize me. I'm a medic. There's sure to be some injuries, someone who tried to eat something they saw a cow eating, or someone having a panic attack and letting her tentacles show. They need to know who to go to."

"Tentacles?" Austin asked. "You were, like, completely naked in the 'Stang. I didn't see any tentacles."

"Just remember what your dick felt like when it was inside me," Ohna answered. "It wasn't just pussy muscles getting you that hard."

"Oh, shit. And you… stuck a finger up my butt," he croaked. "Sort of."

Ohna grinned at him and he blushed red.

They found a booth in the diner with two other people already in it, but they made room for the three to crowd in with them.

"Meta. Nina. These are my friends, Austin and Cece. You might have noticed, Cece and I are twins. I had a rocky road getting here after Orin bounced me out of the shuttle in Texas."

"Ohna? I was expecting a little Dutch girl like Nina," Meta said, pointing at his companion.

"You know what they say: No plan's a good plan. Anyway, I'm here. Have we got any injury reports?" Ohna asked.

"Orin's shuttle finally landed in a cornfield just outside of town. A few of the ones who got tossed from the shuttle in Texas but got back in were pretty banged up. And one proved to be allergic to corn. Kept fading in and out of his human body and showing his tentacles all swollen. We sent him back to the ship. How about you?" Meta asked.

"When I stumbled on Cece, she'd just been shot," Ohna said. "She's fine now. Austin was a little malnourished, but mostly he was just horny."

"You've always been good at curing that," Nina laughed.

"Cece and Austin, you can close your mouths now. I told you we were invading. You're going to meet a lot of us, you know," Ohna said. "This is Meta and Nina. We decided to make the diner our first aid station. We don't expect much serious, but we have to be prepared."

"I'm cool with it," Cece said. "It's just that you guys look so normal. I mean like regular people."

"We plan to stay this way, at least until everyone is established and used to seeing us around. You know, this way people will continue to believe it's all a hoax."

"I'm a believer," Austin said. "What do you want us to do?"

"Have breakfast," Ohna said. "Things will get busy later. It's a great subterfuge to have humans and aliens working together. We'll need you to help handle traffic in and out. Our intelligence says most of the farmers and locals here show up about eight-thirty or nine. Folks who have to go to the city for work are the early ones. If there are scuffles, try to stay out of them. I don't want to have to patch you two up. We have some unfinished business to attend to later!"

HARLAN AND MILLIE got to West-By-God Virginia in record time and Harlan started navigating south of Wheeling by instinct, not even trying to recall the chicken-scratched map he'd originally followed. He just let his muscle memory respond to the curves and turns and soon saw the two tire-tracks into the woods. He started to turn in when he saw the backwoods ho standing in the middle of the track with her shotgun.

"Friends!" Harlan yelled, jumping out of the SUV and waving his arms.

"You!" she yelled. "I won'ed who pickin' m'up." She spat out a wad of what Harlan could only hope was tobacco, then continued in a clear voice. "Okay! Pretty lady up front with you. We'll have some fun on our way."

"Where are we going?" Harlan asked.

"West. Just got the coordinates after they picked up the president," she said pointing skyward.

"Who picked up the president?" Millie demanded with her head out the window.

"Aliens," Harlan and the ho answered together. She laughed and got in the back seat.

"Head up to I-70 and floor it," she said. "We've got to get to Longview, Kansas and if you obey the speed limits, it's thirteen hours. We need to be there in eleven."

Millie felt a hand slide across her shoulder, headed toward her breast.

"I'm Rina. What's your name, cutie?"

"Uh… Millie. Harlan, stop and let me get in back with Rina," Millie said as Rina caressed her breast. She glanced down at the tentacle wrapped around her left nipple. "Right damn now, Harlan!"

Harlan slammed on the brakes and Millie was out the front door and into the back door, wrapped in Rina's warm and sensual grip. Harlan just shook his head and pressed the accelerator. By the time he reached I-70, Millie and Rina were both naked.

"Covfefe," the president muttered as he settled onto the golden throne in the new Air Force One bathroom. "Covfefe."

No one believed him when he was in office the first time. Thought he was crazy. Well, meeting up with goddam aliens will make anyone a little crazy. Now they were back.

He flushed and went into the office, where he sat behind a luxurious rosewood desk, studded with diamonds. Or Rhinestones. Whatever. This office was much better suited to him than the Ovaltine office. It was nice of the Covfefe to arrange the gift from Qatar. They wanted him to be housed in appropriate luxury.

"Bela!" he yelled. The personal assistant on Air Force One hustled into his office from a side room where she was always available. The young woman came as a gift with the airplane. Young! She insisted she was well over eighteen, but she looked so young even Jeffrey would have wanted her.

"Oh, Mr. President," Bela said. "You look so stressed out. Has it been a hard day? Let Bela take care of all your needs."

There was more than one reason he didn't want the first lady or his son on this flight. Bela loosened his tie and unbuttoned his shirt. Her hands were like magic. He hadn't had a hard-on in six years until Bela arrived. Now he was already feeling the wood arising. All he had to do was sit there and Bela would take care of everything else.

"Mr. President, due to the nature of our emergency, we are going radio silent and are turning off the transponder to conceal your location," the pilot said over a speaker on the president's desk. "We will be jamming radar as well."

"Is it that bad?" the president asked. "Well, don't just sit there doing nothing! Make it so!"

He chuckled to himself. He'd always wanted to turn to his Number One and use that line. Of course, the vice president wasn't competent to take that order. He barely kept order in the Senate. And just now, he was carrying a very personal message to the Russians, offering to split the spoils of a conquered Ukraine.

Bela got his trousers unfastened and was doing wonderful things to him. Oh, yes. Wonderful.

The pilot radioed his intent and suddenly vanished out of sight as far as ground control was concerned. The president glanced out the window at the Navy fighter flight accompanying him. It made him feel secure. He wondered how the old fighters were able to keep up with the new jet. A moment later, he fell asleep at his desk. Bela picked him up and tossed him on his bed. That task was done. The twenty office and cabinet members who had managed to keep up with him as he fled the White House and sixteen of the twenty-six crew on the plane also dropped off to sleep right where they were on the plane.

And then the plane disappeared from American airspace.

"THERE'S A SPIKE in use of the AI chat apps," reported Xota on the alien mothership.

"Move another hundred personnel to the response lines. All general dummy responses. If conversations become too intense, claim system overload," Zeta said. Having her people acting as artificial intelligence chat engines had been one of the best moves she'd made in the past decade of preparing for the landing. The chatbots launched by the big social media weren't nearly as sophisticated as people thought they were. They'd been chatting with aliens all this time.

"Air Force One and Flight 19 are arriving in the flight bay in three minutes," Haro said. "I'm going down to meet the team. Anyone else want to go?"

"I'd like to tag along," Darrell said. "I've just got to see that monstrosity he accepted from the Qatari."

"Well, it was delivered by Qatar but we'd actually set it up. Put every little twist in it we could to appeal to his ego. It's actually equipped with our own navigation and propulsion system. Disguising those as standard equipment was the hardest part. We promised the president he could have the plane when we were done with the takeover."

"You mean he's in on it?" Darrell asked.

"Not that he knows," Haro said. "We made the agreement and then erased his memory of it. Still had a couple things slip out. The guy's brain has so much miscellaneous garbage in it that it's a wonder he remembers to breathe. He was pretty easy to convince. The plane and a dozen fifteen-year-old beauty pageant contestants to do his bidding."

"Hey, wait!" Janelle said. "We aren't going to be a party to kidnapping young girls into sexual slavery for that dirty old man!"

"No. Don't worry, honey," Haro said. "It wasn't hard to get volunteers from our people to take on the shape of young girls. There isn't one of the volunteers who's younger than a hundred years old. Half of them aren't even female."

"They're trans?" Janelle asked.

"No. Gender is always kind of fluid for us. It's about time you ate my pussy and felt Zeta's sex tentacle grow in you."

"Oh, that's fine then. Darrell, have you had Zeta's sex tentacle?"

"You bet. Makes me wish we were gender fluid. I'd love to have a pussy and have you stick your dick in me."

"We'll have to figure out a way. After we get your wife and secretary tamed."

Once the behemoth airplane was in the flight bay parked next to DCA1427 and Flight 19, they approached to watch crew members who were unloading the sleeping passengers. A couple dozen other aliens were standing by to strip and examine each of the sleeping passengers. Then they morphed into the shapes, reading memories and dressing in the removed clothing. Darrell thought he recognized the alien dressing as president, but it was still hard for him to tell one alien from another if they weren't in human form. They all looked alike. It was worse than trying to tell one Asian from another in a crowd.

"Well, Darrell, are you ready to take on your new duties as Secretary of State?" the new president asked. Darrell glanced over at the table where the sleeping president was still stretched out naked to be sure it was the alien.

"Yes, sir. I've studied the role and have memorized my lines. I used to be a bit of a thespian, you know. Acted in high school plays and even in a couple musicals in college," Darrell said.

"Good, good. Just do as you're told and we'll get along great."

"I didn't see the first lady get off the plane," Janelle said.

"Can you believe the guy left her and his son asleep in the White House?" Zeta asked. "Works out better this way. The old prez can wake up to his harem of teeny-boppers and we'll fly the first lady in to be with her new husband tomorrow. Life is about to get much better for her."

"Where are you going to store the president?" Darrell asked. "I mean the old president."

"We are people of our word," Haro said. "The reason we created this plane, is because we have a suite on the mothership that is an exact duplicate. We'll move him to it with his bevy of beauties and he'll discover his entire plane is filled with girls for him to seduce, starting with Bela, the attendant who will wake him up."

"I'm amazed you've found so many people willing to have sex with the old goat," Janelle said.

"We have people willing to have sex with every person on earth if they could," Zeta said. "That's why your job as secretary of sex education is so important. We just need to boost the sex drive of humans a little to make them more receptive."

"Is that what you did to me?" Janelle asked as one of the president's tentacles slithered up her leg.

"No, dear. You and Darrell were naturals."

"Yeh gotta come out and see this," Lyle said in the diner at eight o'clock. "Perfect circle burned right in the middle of the corn maze."

"How'd you just happen to discover *that* this morning?" Bert asked.

"Strange doings last night," Lyle said. "Kept seein' a kind of glow flashing by. Thought I was having one of those stroke things. This morning, I had Brett fire up the tractor and we went out to take a look. Perfect crop circle in the middle of that corn maze."

"Did I see Brett drop you off this morning?" one of the regulars asked. "What's he doing driving the tractor into town?"

"Well, we had it fired up. I told the kid he might as well get started with his hayride early and pick kids up for school. They get so damned excited at Halloween."

"True that. With all the news of aliens shooting each other in congress this morning, I'll come take a look at your crop circle. Maybe they've decided to invade Longview," Bert said. Everyone laughed, but they all headed outside to catch Brett and his hay wagon on the next trip by.

"This is perfect!" Ohna said to Austin and Cece. "Catch that wagon. Stick with it and encourage this Brett kid to spend the day picking people up and taking them around. We'll need transportation when the president arrives this evening. Might as well use it to move people around during the day."

"People?" Austin said.

"A few hundred of us landed last night, but we didn't bring cars. Everybody's got to get used to their jobs."

"Got it," Cece said. "Come on, lover. Let's go for a hayride."

Austin and Cece left with the group to go see the crop circle.

7
The Arrival

"**WHERE ARE WE?**" MILLIE asked, a little bewildered. After her last cum at the tentacles of Rina, Millie had passed out and slept for two hours.

"Just crossed the Mississippi into Missouri, darlin'," Harlan said. "It's time for you to drive. I'll pull off for gas at this exit."

"Well, I'm feeling fine, like I just got a good night's sleep. Thank you, Rina."

"It was my pleasure," the alien ho declared. "I just want to get this bad boy into me. We're about five hours from the president's landing and I want to be there to welcome him."

"Five hours all the way across Missouri and half of Kansas?" Millie exclaimed.

"Maybe less if you keep the hammer down," Rina said. "It all depends on how fast you can drive."

"I've got a pilot's license," Millie declared. "I'll *fly* this little truck."

"That's my babe," Harlan declared.

As soon as the tank was filled, Harlan got in the back seat with Rina. By the time Millie had the truck up to 95, Harlan was up in Rina fucking vigorously. After a glance in the rearview mirror, Millie pressed on to 110.

IN LONGVIEW, LITTLE Johnny was having the time of his life. His classmates had been in school since eight, but he'd spent all morning getting in his costume. He was pretty pleased with what he managed to do with a bunch of dryer hose he dug out of a garbage bin and a can of green spray paint. He'd ordered the green alien mask from a Chinese online store all the way back in the summer and had kept it hidden even from his parents.

About noon, he'd headed out to haunt the town. He'd been surprised at the reception he'd received. It seemed like there were a lot more people in town for the holiday than he remembered from the past. But Halloween was a big day in Longview and their reputation was growing with the crowds.

He wandered into Sarah Lee's Diner about noon, thinking he'd yell 'trick or treat!' but the diner was packed and rowdy. People looked like they'd been drinking all day. And they were all in costumes. There was a little jostling going on and a big man tripped over Johnny's flippers. Johnny saw him falling, but couldn't get out of the way. He was knocked out when the big man's weight pinned him to the floor.

WHEN LITTLE JOHNNY woke up, he was lying on the counter and a beautiful woman was bending over him. She had a strange red cross on her bonnet, but otherwise she looked like a girl from one of the videos his father liked to watch before bed. Then another girl who looked exactly the same but with no red cross leaned in from the other side. Johnny found it hard to breathe and pulled at the latex mask until he had it off.

"Oh! You're a human!" the red cross girl said. "What a great costume. I thought you were one of ours."

"If you want, ma'am. But I'm only twelve," Johnny said, a little hopeful.

"You're a perfect little gentleman alien," Ohna laughed. "You're perfect for the wagon. Don't you think so, Cece?"

"Absolutely. Why aren't you in school, kiddo?" Cece asked.

"I got suspended for a day because I made a joke about illegal aliens," Johnny said truthfully.

"I don't see anything wrong with that. Technically, I guess we are."

"You're an alien?" Johnny asked.

He suddenly figured it all out. He'd been knocked out and he was having a big dream he'd wake up from soon. He hoped it wouldn't be like the dreams he had when he spied on his father's videos. That would be embarrassing if he woke up in a crowded restaurant with… He glanced around and realized he really *was* in a crowded restaurant and one of the pretty girls was showing him a tentacle.

Johnny passed out again.

The next time he woke up, the other pretty girl was giving him a glass of water a sip at a time. A nice guy was supporting him from the other side.

"You're really aliens," Johnny said, wide-eyed.

"Not us," Cece said. "Ohna and most of these others are. Seems they got confused about humans eating at noon and all showed up here at the same exact time. No matter how crazy advanced they are, they still have a lot to learn. How would you like a job?"

"I was just getting a head start on trick or treating," Johnny said.

"I'll get you all your favorite candies and Ohna will pay you, too," said the guy. "I'm Austin. We've been riding the hay wagon out to the corn maze and crop circle all morning. We could teach you to be the tour guide. You know a high school kid named Brett? He's driving the tractor with his girlfriend, Bridget."

"I know Brett."

"Okay. All you have to do is ride in the front of the hay wagon in your costume and tell people about the aliens landing out in the corn maze."

"I don't know anything about that!"

"No problem. Cece and me will be with you and give you ideas. You can just make up everything. That's what we've been doing."

"Okay."

That began Johnny's new job as a tour guide.

"Idiots!" Oswald growled as he put an AR15 on top of the stack of firearms beside him. He might not have time to reload when the action started. "We're being invaded and they're playing trick or treat! Going out to look at crop circles without imagining what was causing them."

The last wagonload of people going out to the maze even had a little alien acting like a tour guide. The laughing teenagers thought it was just a kid in a costume. It was a real goddam alien! At least that's what Oswald thought. He'd be watching for that one when the shooting started.

Oswald had gotten a call at eight-thirty in the morning Central Time. Number Fifty-one activated the calling tree. He was located on top of a mountain in West Virginia and kept track of where the president and vice president were at any given time.

'Code name Cheeto' had taken off from DC a little after eight in the morning Eastern Time. Oswald had to write the times down on a sheet of paper with the time zones written on it so he wouldn't subtract an hour when he was supposed to add one. Cheeto left at eight Eastern, seven Central. An hour later at nine Central… no, nine Eastern, the president's new plane disappeared over West Virginia—right where DCA1427 was lost a few days before.

Conclusion: The president had been abducted by aliens. It was as clear as the nose on your face. All eighty-four members of the American Protection Exchange Service—APES—had been put on alert by eight-forty-five. Central time. By noon, Oswald had hay bales stacked in front of his gate, had painted his face in camo, was sitting in a hunting chair on his front porch with a stack of guns beside him, and had drunk a six-pack from the cooler. He was ready.

The phone had been ringing all morning. He'd found out 'Cheeto's Lay' had been hustled into the White House bunker with the crown prince and a dozen secret service agents, which should keep her safe or at least occupied for the rest of the day. Samosa Sam was reported to be in Russia, which was a good place for him. Gunfire had died down in the Capitol and the Army was picking up bodies and survivors. Both were being shipped to a retention center in Florida.

The thing was, no one knew where the aliens would land or exactly when. He hated this part. All he could do was wait, drink, and pray that they'd come to Longview.

As THE DAY wore on, kids got out of school in their costumes and visitors to the town increased. It wasn't unheard of for the population of Longview to double by dinnertime.

The Methodist, Baptist, Lutheran, Catholic, and Presbyterian churches all had long tables set up and were prepared to serve their church specialties. The Methodists had huge kettles of chili cooking. They would serve it with corn chips and coffee or soft drinks. All for just $20.

The Baptists had the grills fired up and would soon be serving hot dogs and hamburgers, garnished with ketchup, onion, tomatoes, mayo, and mustard. And sweet pickle relish. They, too, served soft drinks and potato chips. All for just $20.

The Lutherans, of course, served barbecued pork on a bun, potato salad and baked beans. All for just $20. Beer and wine were available for $20 a glass. At the Presbyterian Church, a vast array desserts, crafted by the women of the community, whether they were members of that church or not. Dessert with coffee, hot or cold, was just $20.

Oh. The Catholics. Under a temporary license from the town, they operated a full bar. Any cocktail the priests could make was available for just $20. For beer or wine, see the Lutherans.

On the outskirts of town, the Pentecostals and Evangelicals were locked in their churches praying.

There was one other church. Next to the town cemetery was the former Episcopalian Church. Those folks built the first church in Longview back in the 1870s when the town was overrun with cowboys and outlaws. It founded the cemetery to deal with the blossoming needs of the frontier railroad and cattle town. They built a monstrously huge brick building, paid for by the diocese and a few cattle barons. It only lasted about 100 years before it closed its doors for all but funerals.

And Halloween.

With so many dead people having passed through its doors, it's not surprising that it acquired a reputation of being haunted. So, it was only natural to open its doors on

Halloween as a haunted house—or church. There was a small haunted house for children set up by the high school kids in the elementary school. As soon as school was out for the day, the older kids went to work decorating the gym with spooky cobwebs, caskets, and ghosts. The Episcopal Church, though, was for adults only.

This year, Darrell's secretary, Kristin, was recruited for the haunted church. She was too young the previous year, as she'd not yet turned eighteen. She'd had a major celebration with Darrell on her birthday back in May, while Stacy was seven months pregnant. She thought she was pretty hot. Stacy even thought so. They'd had a heart-to-heart and a tongue-to-cunt talk after the baby was born.

The church event was more of a show than a typical haunted house. No one went there to see the Holy Ghost, though one year it reportedly showed up. The organizers decorated, dividing the space into isolated areas that could not be seen from each other. People who paid their $20 admission followed a path from one tableau or short scene to the next. Each tableau was a risqué scene featuring various Halloween characters.

A pirate scene featured a knockoff of a famous amusement ride, but with costumes that didn't cover as much, and some action that was definitely not 'family entertainment'—unless you were thinking of starting one. Witches danced around a cauldron in a *Macbeth* parody. In their scene, though, the witches and Mac both lost their clothes and enacted a sexy scene as they danced around the pot. One of the perennial favorites was a reenactment of the masked robbery of the bank that found all the bank employees masked, too. By the end of the night, all clothes except the masks had been removed and bandits were making regular deposits. There were scenes of cowboys and Indians, a wizarding school, ghosts, ghouls, vampires, a few undefined monsters, and this year, space aliens.

That was a last-minute addition when the news broke, and Kristin had been recruited or volunteered for the scene. Stacy had agreed to help with the scene, but with her husband missing, there was always the chance she wouldn't show up. If she did show up, so much the better. Two beautiful naked teenage girl aliens would be much better than just one.

The whole church was a kind of maze through which people would wander, coming upon a scene and stopping to gaze at the mostly naked actors. Of course, they were all made up and fully disguised so no one could recognize them—even each other. Very few people on the organizing committee knew who was in which tableau. For days after Halloween, people would wander around looking at their neighbors and trying to decide if they'd seen them naked or possibly even fucked them.

It was all the out-of-towners who ponied up the $20 admission to spend an hour or so watching the spectacle. They were all warned upon admission that they could be touched by any of the characters and interaction would be guided. The closer to midnight it came, the more daring the acts and the audience participation became. The event made so much money for the town that they didn't have any local taxes.

Kristin rushed to Stacy's house through the crowds after work to get dressed and made up to go to the old church for the nine o'clock show. Stacy was waiting for her.

"I'm so nervous," Kristin said. "You did it last year. Will it be okay?"

"Of course it will," Stacy answered. "I'll be right there with you. Without Darrell, we'll have to grab someone else. Maybe the mayor. Or your father!"

"Stacy! I couldn't!" Kristin cried.

"Oh, yeah. Maybe we'll find a well-hung visitor. Just don't start fucking too soon. If you start at nine, you won't be able to walk in the morning."

"I wish Darrell was here," Kristin sighed.

"The bastard has been screwing an OF model," Stacy replied. "He'll show up with his tail between his legs soon enough. Now strip down and let's work on that beautiful body of yours."

"You really don't mind me screwing Darrell?" Kristin asked.

"Hmm. I thought I'd be pissed. And he thinks so. But as long as you get your face between my legs on a regular basis, I'll tolerate it."

Stacy stripped her own clothes off and embraced Kristin. They kissed until they were both panting and had their hands all over each other. Kristin pushed Stacy down on the bed and spread her legs.

"How could I not want to dive into this pussy. You taste like honey," Kristin said, taking a long and sensual lick.

"Yes! Get that tongue to work, little bitch. Momma needs a big one. Yes! Get your fingers in me. I want it! You'll figure it out eventually. A dick is nice for that full feeling it gives you, but there's nothing like a girl's tongue. Get up here and let me taste you while you're doing me. I want my tongue in your twat."

Eventually the two got out of each other's pussy and into their makeup so they were unrecognizable, and Stacy turned on the TV. It was six o'clock and time for the news.

"It's been a tumultuous day in America," The newscaster said.

"Civil unrest broke out early this morning in Washington DC as the president alluded to an alien invasion. A flight of navy fighters, missing for 80 years, landed at Andrews Air Force Base. It escorted Air Force One into the air and an hour later disappeared again. The president has been out of touch since a declaration that he would personally negotiate with the aliens, who he calls Covfefe.

*"The last word of the president's address to the nation
this morning was that he would negotiate directly with the
Covfefe and would bring the invasion to an end by dinnertime. You may remember, the president promised to end the
Ukraine war in a day; it is still under way.*

*"The vice president is also in the air, someplace between
Russia and the United States, and is therefore unable to
act in the president's absence. The next in line would be the
speaker of the house, but it is unclear how many congressmen
and senators survived today's violence across the aisle, and
how many are still on vacation while the government is
closed down. ICE has promised that survivors, transported
to Florida, would be questioned and examined to determine
their status as American citizens or alligator food.*

*"This leaves a question of who is actually in charge, as
most cabinet members have been isolated in the White House
bunker."*

The newscaster paused and held a hand to his ear.

*"This just in! A plane from Flight 19, missing for eighty
years until this morning when it arrived to escort Air Force
One to its meeting with the aliens, has just landed in a small
Midwestern town where a local broadcaster is covering a
Halloween event. We go live to Jerome Cavendish of KNKD
in Longview, Kansas. Jerome, what can you tell us?"*

"This is Jerome Cavendish, live from the Halloween Capital
of the world, Longview, Kansas, where a Navy fighter plane
missing for eighty years has landed. Pilot Charles Taylor is
approaching now. Lieutenant Taylor, what can you tell us about
your past eighty years?"

"Not much," said the pilot. "No time passed at all for us.

But what is more important is that we have been escorting the President of the United States and he has selected this as his landing spot. We will expect the first of his entourage on approach now."

"Who is the first of his entourage?" asked the excited newsman.

"We were informed this is flight DCA1427," said the pilot.

People saw the approaching aircraft coming fast and scattered to hide. Others who had heard the news bulletins began arriving. DCA1427 was a wide-body jumbo jet that required at least three miles of perfect runway to land. The Longview airport, such as it was, was a half-mile dirt track.

The plane came in fast, drew to a stop in midair, and settled gently on the runway, right behind the fighter. Before people could comprehend what was happening, two more fighters streaked in and landed behind the passenger plane. Then the sparkling, jewel-encrusted visage of Air Force One landed, with two more fighters behind it. That pretty much occupied all the space on the dirt runway.

A portable hay conveyor was rolled up to the jumbo jet. The doors were opened and people began to emerge.

"WE MADE IT!" Millie yelled. She didn't let up on the accelerator.

"Straight through town to the airport," Rina said.

Millie started backing off the speed as she spotted the crowds gathering. Amazingly, the crowd parted for the Bronco and they pulled up in front of the airplanes.

"That's Air Force One!" Millie screamed, wondering why they'd been allowed so close. Passengers were flooding out of the other plane and down the conveyor. Everyone was hurrying to join the Navy pilots lining up to welcome the president.

"And that's DCA1427," Harlan added. "Will wonders never cease."

"THAT ROTTEN SON of a bitch!" Stacy screamed. "That filthy mother fucking cock sucker."

Kristin stared at the TV.

"Is that really Darrell being escorted by the beautiful flight attendant?"

"And the OF model he's been fucking," Stacy said. "Where's my gun? Oswald left me one the other day. That shit has a surprise waiting for him if he thinks he can just walk in here with another bitch or two. I'll blast his balls off and he can spend his life watching us fuck his new toys."

"You make me so hot, Stacy. Fuck me again!"

BRETT PULLED UP with his hay wagon in front of Air Force One, but he and Bridget stayed in the tractor cab making out. The door of the big plane opened, dropping stairs to the wagon. Cece, Little Johnny, and Austin were still on the wagon, expecting to pick up another load of passengers for the corn maze. It was just getting to be dark and a couple of big farm trucks shone their lights on the makeshift platform.

Ohna ran to meet them and almost bowled her mother over as they collided and bumped into Darrell, Janelle, and Haro. They all jumped up to the wagon and stood respectfully next to the stairs.

"Mama, this is Austin, Cece, and Johnny," Ohna said. "We kind of fell in together when I fell out."

"You sure chose a pretty girl for your model," Zeta said. "I hope they are as good as they look." Zeta hugged Austin and Cece, sniffing deeply. "Oh, yes," she sighed. "This is Darrell and Janelle. They've been very helpful. And you, Johnny. How are you doing on this Halloween?"

"I'm having fun, Mrs. Alien," he said. "I tell people all about the crop circle and alien culture."

"I would love to hear that."

Just then 'Hail to the Chief' started playing from speakers on the airplane. A moment later the president stood at the top of the stairs and waved at the crowd. The three or four thousand mixed townspeople, visitors, and aliens might have been the largest crowd the president had ever spoken to. Too bad the only crowd he saw were half a dozen young beauties he could grab by the pussy.

8
Happy Halloween

THE PRESIDENT KEPT WAVING as he descended the stairs and approached the microphone hastily set up for him.

"What a great country this is," he said. "I was just saying to my family this morning how great America is. The greatest. Probably the greatest that's ever been. In fact, we're going to quit referring to athletes as the goat. America is the goat. We're the greatest of all time.

"I know a lot of you were doubting that because of the panic our legislators and judges tried to instill this morning. It shows how clueless most of our so-called leaders were. I said were because after they panicked and started shooting at each other and at good American citizens, we had Marines go in and clean up the mess. Don't worry about them anymore. It shows what happens when all we ever get is fake news. I tried to settle things down, but these were mentally ill people who shouldn't have been on the streets.

"Now when I found out about the so-called invasion from outer space—fake news. There was no invasion. Or if there was it was all a big mistake and they didn't mean it that way. But the Democrats—and, I'm sorry to say a lot of misinformed and gullible Republicans—had to go tell people the end of the world was coming. They're just looking out for themselves and don't really care about the American people like I do. I care about real Americans and I see thousands in front of me right here in Longview, Kansas.

"When I was told the situation, I went straight to the source. That's right. I flew up in the wonderful airplane that our Qatari allies gifted to the presidency. We've responded by giving the Qatari a base in Idaho. I had our top pilots, and these brave men of Flight 19—people, give a hand to these brave pilots who crossed time to escort me—our best people flew me right up into the… up there, and I demanded an immediate meeting with the Covfefe supreme commander. I know a lot about being the supreme commander. I'm the commander in chief of the greatest military on earth. No one knows about command better than I do.

"Commander Geti was all too happy to see me. We have a lot in common. He asked me to bring my wife and daughter on my next trip. Big fan of the family. Wants to meet them all. Commander Geti and I sat together for hours. We talked about the world and what his race could do to improve things here on earth. And then I asked him the hard questions. I said 'Commander, what are you going to do about the fine people of DCA1427? What do I need to do to have you return these people?' And do you know what he said? 'Nothing.' It was all just a silly mistake. Cultural anomaly.

"They just wanted to get to know some people from our great country so they'd know how to talk to us. And I met these people, right there on the mothership. Good people. They were all helping Covfefe to understand our people. Smart people, mostly from right here in the heartland. I met them, and the first thing I thought—the very first thing—was I need some of these people on my staff. We need to reform the government and drain the swamp of Washington DC once and for all.

"And so, I'm announcing some very important people for my new cabinet members. First and foremost, a man who truly understands the American people from right here in Longview, Darrell Gwinner, will be my new Secretary of State. We can't have congress affirm him, because they're all gone. He'll be the first of my cabinet members.

"Then, I've selected a popular young woman from Kansas City, Janelle Cummbridge, as our new Secretary of Education. You know we got rid of the old and corrupt Department of Education. Now it's time to rebuild a department that is prepared for the twenty-first century. And since Janelle was born in this century, there is no one better to introduce a new kind of education that will prepare the nation to embrace new social standards and get our bodies to catch up with our minds.

"There are many more. My new press secretary, Zeta. My new Secretary of Health, Ohna. Our new chief of staff, Haro. And many of the others who just flew in with us here. And that brings us to our final announcement for this Halloween evening. While the Army and Marines finish cleaning house and clearing out Washington DC, we are declaring Longview Kansas as our new emergency capital of the United States of America. Welcome to the new heart of America."

The president's speech ended to tumultuous cheers. He waved and invited the one lone reporter and his cameraman into Air Force One. They were followed by Rina, Millie, and Harlan. Once they were in the plane, the stairs were retracted and the door closed.

"Damn him!" Stacy yelled at Kristin. "He thinks he can just waltz in here with his secretary of special education and just... just..."

"Fuck us?" Kristin asked hopefully.

"Of course he can fuck us!" Stacy breathed. "The right-hand man of the president! I bet you Darrell convinced him to move to Longview. It's just like him. But he has to bow down and worship this pussy."

"Do you think he'll get here before we have to get over to the church?"

"Of course he will. He knows what's important. He's probably on his way now. We need to be ready. Let's finish our makeup."

DARRELL WAS, INDEED, on his way home in the hay wagon with those who had been with the president. First, Brett dropped Johnny off at home and admonished him to be inside by nine o'clock. Then they stopped in front of Oswald Kennedy's compound. Hay bales were still stacked inside the locked gates and Oswald was on his porch.

"Oswald Kennedy, America needs your house to be a place where the president can live," Haro called out from the gate.

Now, since Oswald had no television or radio, and he hadn't had a call in a while, he was unaware of the president's arrival or his typically disjointed speech. He saw a guy dressed as a pilot and assumed the worst.

"You can't fool me!" he yelled. "Dirty illegal alien scum!"

With that, he opened fire.

It was a surprise attack and Haro reflexively fired his ray gun back. It went through the lock on the gate, melting it, setting the hay bales on fire, and straight through Oswald. Result expected.

"Medic!" Haro screamed. "Negotiations complete."

Ohna leapt off the wagon, rushing to Haro and tearing his

clothes open where the rifle rounds had exposed large amounts of alien skin and green blood. She opened her hip pouch and went to work.

Cece and Austin rushed the gate with Cece's .45 drawn. They pushed through the flaming bales and Darrell rushed past them. He ran to Oswald on the porch.

"Medic!" he screamed, but it was too late to do anything for Oswald by the time Zeta reached him.

Janelle acted quickly on the other side of the wagon, grabbing an alien named Lado, the co-pilot of her plane.

"You have to take a different body, quickly!" she whispered, pointing him to the house.

It wouldn't do to have a resident of the town killed. They could get away with just about anything or anyone else. The alien rushed to the porch where Darrell was still looking in shock at the dead survivalist. They quickly went to work, stripping his clothes and multiple weapons. The alien assessed the body and began the morphing transformation.

Zeta and Ohna helped Haro back onto the wagon. He would recover thanks to Ohna's quick removal of the bullets and application of healing remedies. She joined Cece and Austin on the porch with the new Oswald. Half a dozen other aliens extinguished the fire and hid Oswald's body for disposal in the morning. They went into the house to assess the situation and prepare for the president's arrival the next day. They would have their work cut out for them. The place was almost unlivable—even for an alien—and looked like it had never been cleaned.

Darrell, Janelle, Haro, and Zeta continued on to Darrell's house, leaving a sizable crew to clean up the mess in the compound. Brett dropped them off about a quarter till eight, then he and Bridget picked up Sheldon, Elaine, and a dozen classmates for a trip to the corn maze as if nothing had interrupted their Halloween plans. Someone was going to get laid tonight.

ACTUALLY, THERE WERE a lot of people who planned to get laid that night. Darrell welcomed Zeta, Haro, and Janelle into his home. He led them directly upstairs and burst into his bedroom with Zeta right behind.

"Honey, I'm home!" he called before he fully grasped the import of the two naked female figures with stylized alien makeup on and a gun in the hand of one.

"You bastard!" Stacy screamed. "I'll shoot your balls off if there's anything left of them."

After the incident with Oswald, Zeta didn't hesitate to act. A tentacle sprang out to slap the gun away as another tentacle raised a blaster. Darrell knocked the ray gun away and it blasted a hole in the bedroom wall.

"Stop!" Darrell shouted.

"A... It... Tentac..." Stacy sputtered.

"Alien!" Kristin finished.

"You know I love it when you greet me naked," Darrell said, squeezing his wife close enough to get two fistfuls of her tits as he drove his tongue into her mouth. She was soon responding with a hand on his balls and the gun lying somewhere on the floor. Darrell pulled away and dragged eighteen-year-old Kristin into an equally passionate embrace.

They parted eventually to see Darrell's three companions standing agape.

"Oh, yeah. These are our three new family members, Janelle, Zeta, and Haro. They'll be living with the three of us now."

"Three of us?" the two young women chorused.

"Yes. Stacy, Kristin will be living with us now, too."

"Oh. Of course she will. We planned that, anyway," Stacy said.

"We did?" Kristin asked.

"Yeah. I just hadn't told you yet. But why are these… people here?" Stacy demanded.

"These are our new lovers," Darrell said. "I had to assume you saw the video of Janelle and me. You wasted no time posting one of your own. Was that Bert Beeson? Dude is hung like a horse!"

"But the aliens?" Kristin squeaked.

Darrell moved closer to her with an arm wrapped securely around her. He stroked her breasts and torso. Janelle mimicked the same with Stacy.

"Haven't you ever imagined being held so you can't move while a tentacled creature crawls across your naked body and you're helpless to resist as one of the slimy tentacles finds your hot wet sex and begins to explore it? At first you feel it just sliding around, and then it tickles your little clitty. It strokes it like the most sensual tongue you've ever imagined, getting you closer and closer, until it opens your pussy and pokes just inside. You feel it moving in farther like it's growing right inside you until you don't think anything else can fit. Then… only then does it begin to slide in and out of your hot hole, filling you and leaving you empty until you're sure you'll burst with excitement. And just when you can't take anymore, it swells and gushes into your cunt."

"Yes! Oh, God yes. I'm cumming!" Kristin and Stacy both cried out.

Haro and Zeta had been following Darrell's narrative and applying a tentacle to each of them until the climax. They slowly withdrew from the panting women as Darrell and Janelle held them.

"And now you know why they're here," Darrell whispered.

Kristin and Stacy fell into deep kisses with Haro and Zeta.

"Oh my God! We've got to get to the church!" Kristin cried. "We'll be late."

"BUT MR. PRESIDENT," Jerome Cavendish from KNKD asked in the presidential conference room aboard Air Force One, "don't you need more security, out here in the wilds of Kansas? I only see a couple of Secret Service guys and the fellows carrying the football. It can't be safe here!"

The reporter had been accompanied on board by his cameraman and three other people he hadn't been introduced to yet. They were still broadcasting a live stream after the exclusive tour of the aircraft.

"Jerome… Can I call you Jerry, Jerry? Jerry, what better protection against all our ills than the good honest people of America? I have decent people all around me. What further Protection can a true American need than the love of the American people? Now take Rina here," he said referring to the West Virginia ho for the first time. "100% genuine American, here on the plane to serve me. And here's…" He paused, not knowing their names.

"Millie and Harlan, Mr. President," Rina supplied. The couple were still in their bathrobes as they'd been when they rushed out of Millie's apartment in the morning. *I should have brought a towel,* Harlan thought.

"Millie and Harlan," the president said without missing a beat. "Two hardworking Americans who are here after facing all kinds of ad… ad… difficulty. We're going to tell their story later, but it was a really difficult difficulty. The most difficult. I am going to invite them to share a luxurious bed tonight here on Air Force One. They deserve that, and they'll be working in the new capital, right here in Longview."

Harlan and Millie looked at Rina and she grinned back. They shrugged.

"Now, Jer… You don't mind if I call you Jer… it's time to wrap it up tonight. Get out there in this beautiful Halloween night in Longview and enjoy yourself. Meet me tomorrow morning and we'll go look at the site for the new golf course. We'll turn this place into the Midwest Mar-a-Lago. Great. It will be great like America."

As soon as the reporter was off the plane, the president folded Rina in tentacle-like arms and the two practically melted into one.

"Oh, Toto, it's been too long since we were together."

"Welcome to Kansas, Rina."

"I already introduced Harlan and Millie. We drove all the way from West Virginia to get here after we took the plane up. They're wonderful."

"Millie and Harlan, I meant what I said. Come on upstairs to the presidential bed and join my first lady and me."

"It will be a pleasure Mr. President," they said.

"Oh, it sure will be."

ALL THE PLAYERS arrived at the haunted church by eight-thirty. Everyone was masked and costumed so no one knew who their neighbors were. They'd spend the next few days wondering who they had felt up or possibly even fucked while in disguise. Of course, the secrecy was often a sham. It wasn't unusual for people to arrange an assignation during the three-hour event.

That was what happened to Stacy just a year ago. She'd made sure Oswald knew she was playing Little Bo Peep in a pastoral scene that had a lot of sheep copulating. Oswald arrived as Little Boy Blue—a stretch for his age, but he had a full head mask—and pulled Stacy under the haystack where they stayed connected for a long time. The result was little Cray, who Darrell thought was his since he'd been fucking his new wife pretty steadily. At the time of the crime, though, Darrell was balls deep in Josephine Carlisle, the clerk at the Dollar General who was playing Mary with her little lamb.

It was an honest mistake.

This year, though, the entire Gwinner clan planned to put on a hot alien scene. Darrell, Stacy, Kristin, Janelle, Zeta, and Haro could hardly keep their hands—or tentacles—off each other. This was going to give a decidedly x-rating to the concept of alien invasion. Having two actual aliens in the mix would enhance the look and feel. They expected people to be lined up wanting to participate with them.

A little hands-on entertainment.

Patience Plunkett had been in charge of recruiting the act leaders this year. Usually, the person in charge of the haunted house started with key individuals. Then those individuals recruited their own teams for their vignette and informed Patience of their theme. She'd recruited Kristin and was worried that she would never get a theme for her station.

On Monday, Kristin had reported her theme selection: alien invasion. Two days later, nearly every team leader preparing a vignette had requested an alien theme, but the subject was taken. Patience turned them all down. She was rather looking forward to seeing the eighteen-year-old in her first sex scene. Of course, the team leader was not *required* to be in the scene. Patience had never seen an eighteen-year-old leader who didn't jump at the chance to get naked in front of a few hundred people. She couldn't blame them. She'd done a Star Wars theme as harem Leia who gradually lost her flimsy costume to Jabba when she was eighteen. Ronnie, playing Jabba, had convinced her that night that she should marry him.

Everyone was in position and the first hundred people had paid their $20 and were in line to enter when the doors opened at nine o'clock sharp. Many out-of-towners rushed to be among the first admitted, not realizing the shows tended to get more explicit as the night wore on. Not that there weren't plenty of bare boobs and a few dangling sausages to see earlier, but there was a much higher chance that an audience member would get to feel some exposed flesh, expose some themselves, and even get intimate with cast members later.

In addition to those recruited for the main vignette, extras were also recruited. They dressed in costumes and masks consistent with the theme, but they stepped out of shadows, from behind set pieces, and even dropped from the ceiling to surprise audience members, often with intimate contact.

It was *possible* the haunted church might not blossom into a full-blown orgy, but unlikely.

There was a surprise waiting for many people this night. Much of it centered on the alien invasion area. Aliens kept popping out of unexpected areas, often pulling an unsuspecting spectator through a passage where a change took place. An audience member was extracted, stripped, and used as a pattern for the alien to adopt his or her shape, then dress in the costume. The audience member was moved into a waiting van for transport to a shuttle for storage.

Gradually, the town's population shifted to being aliens rather than humans.

"D, I KNEW you'd be back. I never quit believing. It's almost midnight. Let me have it, baby. Put it in me!" Kristin moaned as Darrell caressed her green dyed breasts. She bent over their spaceship and he moved up behind her.

"Oh, babycakes! I don't care how many women and aliens you bring home with you. I'm yours, all yours. Take me, Darrell.

Spread me out and plant your flag," Stacy said to her husband. He laid her out on a space couch, pushed her legs back to her breasts, and lined himself up at her opening.

"Mmm. Alien tentacles are really great, but sometimes, all I want is your man-size dick. Stick it in me, DG. Do it like we did on the airplane," Janelle said as Darrell stood behind her, rubbing his dick up and down her crack. It caught on her wet hole and began to slowly sink into her.

At five minutes until midnight, three Darrells in identical masks, with identical naked bodies, thrust into the three masked women simultaneously with two of them having no idea their mate was a shapeshifting alien.

BRETT DROPPED OFF the last of the teens who had been to the corn maze and the tractor putted back to the barn. Still on the bed of straw in the trailer, Sheldon and Elaine were removing the last of their clothes. In the cab of the tractor, Bridget had been naked for the past hour. She was bent over Brett's cock sucking as he brought the tractor to a stop in the barn.

"It's time for you to have some fun," Brett said. "You've been keeping me hard all evening and I really want to fuck now. But not until I make sure you've cum at least twice."

"Twice? Brett, can you do that?" Bridget exclaimed.

"If I can't, I'm going to give up on sex because I'll be no kind of man," Brett bragged.

The two left the cab and climbed into the trailer, narrowly missing stepping on Sheldon's bare ass as he bounced in and out of Elaine. She was moaning loudly. Bridget stopped to stare at them for a moment before Brett dragged her down on a blanket and began kissing and sucking on her. He hadn't even moved between her legs when she had her first orgasm, just from having him suck on her nipples and maul her breasts. She'd been working up to this all evening.

When he parted her legs and started licking her pussy, she gyrated so much he had trouble maintaining contact. Her moan grew in volume until she screeched out her next cum. Brett didn't stop, figuring he had a good thing going. It was only a few minutes before she'd ramped up to another big one.

"My God! What did you do to her?" Elaine gasped, looking over to the other blanket. It was pretty dark in the barn, so she couldn't clearly see what position they were in.

"Elly! He's licking my clit. I've never felt anything like it. I'm going to cum again!" Bridget gasped, rising to yet another big orgasm. She screamed out her pleasure so loudly, Brett was afraid his father would hear them from inside the house.

Of course, Lyle wasn't in the house. He and a curvaceous woman he met in the church while performing in the old cowboys and Indians scene were still locked in an embrace while the last of the visitors were being guided out the main doors. His lover had the most talented pussy he'd ever encountered, milking him of everything he had. Well, Lyle was a single dad and saw no reason he shouldn't take this hot piece home with him. Soon.

"You!" Elaine shouted at Sheldon. "Get your face down between my legs and start licking or I'm going over to Brett!"

Sheldon didn't want his night of fucking to end on that kind of a note, so he got his face between Elaine's legs and started licking, even though his cum was running out of her hole.

Bridget was clawing at Brett after her fourth cum, trying to get him up to fill her pussy with his cock. Brett was more than happy to slide into her wet mess and the two started fucking vigorously, both cumming noisily.

It was scarcely one o'clock. They figured they had a few more hours of entertaining each other before they'd have to go to sleep.

9
Alien Nation

ALL SAINTS' DAY DAWNED on a sleepy and somwhat hungover Longview, Kansas, a couple of hours later than on Washington, DC. Things were quiet in DC. Janitors and a few remaining staff moved into the Capitol to clean up the blood and gore under the watchful supervision of military personnel.

The Chief Justice of the Supreme Court sent out a recorded message encouraging people to remain calm and know the constitution was still the law of the land. Then he disappeared.

No one was shooting in the streets. Loud speakers mounted on squeaky tanks warned that armed citizens in the streets would be shot and arrested. Most businesses remained closed. It appeared the only functioning government entities remaining were the Smithsonian Institution and the Public Library. Everything else had been closed for a month.

Similar scenes played out in cities across the country as it awoke.

Not so in Longview. Overnight, dozens of executive orders were issued via social media in 140-character bursts. The president emerged from his jewel-encrusted airplane with three personal advisors, Rina, Harlan, and Millie. They rode on a hay wagon driven by a naked Brett with his equally naked girlfriend

Bridget. They picked up Jerome, the news reporter, and his cameraman and went out to the corn maze where the president announced development of his new Capital Golf Course would begin in the next week. Lyle met them out there and signed a bill of sale for the property.

Then they went to the new presidential residence, which had been made over during the night into a palatial structure behind a brick wall with slightly melted gates. Austin, Cece, and Ohna met the president there and introduced a very reasonable facsimile of Oswald Kennedy to welcome him to his new residence.

While standing on the steps of the house, the president announced a new constitutional convention to begin in thirty days. In that time, states were to elect their delegates and a convention center would be built in Longview.

"We'll have a full convention center built by then, next to the golf course," the president said. "It will have the best ballroom the country has ever seen. Whole new meaning to the term ballroom."

And all that happened before eight in the morning. The president had never looked so fit before. He promised the country would be renewed stronger and richer than ever.

In Sarah Lee's Diner, people who had woken up in various states of undress and/or sexual positions, were dragging themselves in to get coffee and breakfast. Josephine Carlisle, the clerk at Dollar General, slid into a booth to recover from her role as a witch in the Macbeth scene at the haunted church. A bewildered Lado, in the guise of Oswald Kennedy, looked around and she waved him over to sit opposite her.

"Doing okay, Oswald?" she asked.

"A little… um… bewildered. Things took an unexpected turn last night."

"No kidding," Josephine said.

Josephine was a little bewildered herself. She'd lost track of how many orgasms she'd been given while bent over the cauldron last night as a naked witch. She was sure Oswald had been the cause of one of them. They'd been in costumes and masks, of course. She'd been speculating about him, though.

"What do you think about the aliens? Think any of them are here in Longview?" Oswald asked.

"Hmph!" Josephine responded. "Wishful thinking. At the rate I'm going, I'm more likely to meet an alien than the love of my life."

A few faces in the diner turned toward her, but looked away when they saw she was with Oswald.

"So, uh…," Oswald began, motioning with his hand a little because he had no idea who he was talking to. He hadn't reached the body quickly enough to gather any but the most surface memories—mostly of shooting at Haro.

"Josephine. You are bewildered, Oswald," she laughed. He was a strange one, but she always had a fascination for him. And they weren't getting any younger.

"Are you seeing anyone now?" Oswald asked.

"You mean dating, a therapist, or hallucinations?" she asked. Oswald stared at her.

"Yeah. I guess. I mean, I'd like to, you know, see if you like me. I mean to go out. On dates. And stuff."

"Oswald, how did you get a reputation as the town tough guy?" she asked. "You sound like a teenager. I don't need to work today. Want to go see if we're compatible?"

"Yeah. I mean, that's what I was thinking."

What Lado had actually been thinking was that he missed all the fun the previous night because he'd been rushed in to take on the body of Oswald Kennedy, who had been stupid enough to shoot at Haro. Any one of the aliens would have responded the same way. It felt primitive to be carrying around a couple of Oswald's guns when he could fire his ray gun faster than he could draw the old-fashioned pistols. He'd come to the diner just to see if any fun was yet to be had.

Josephine definitely looked like fun to be had. They finished breakfast and Oswald escorted her to the presidential palace, which was far more palatial inside than anyone in Longview suspected, due to the work of all the aliens under Cece and Austin's direction.

It wasn't going to be a bad day at all.

THE OFFICIAL PRESIDENTIAL address to the press waited until they'd all arrived and set up cameras in front of the 'palace.' The public was surprised at the commanding presence of the president.

"When you went to the polls a year ago this coming Tuesday, you voted for a promise of radical reform. Common sense in government. Cutting the expenses of big government. And getting rid of the corruption.

"Overnight… Well, I guess it's been two days now. It depends on how you count it. Most things happened between yesterday and today, so that is overnight. Overnight, we've eliminated the corruption in Washington, DC. This wasn't getting rid of a little of it. We reduced corruption and government waste by a thousand percent. Maybe three thousand percent. We got rid of more corruption than anyone knew we had.

"We brought our newly cleaned house to our new capital city of Longview, Kansas. Wonderful people here in Longview. The heart of America. This is where food comes from. Just this morning I went out to walk through a field of corn that will become one of the most beautiful golf courses in the world in just a few short months. It will be better than any golf course that's ever been. People will come from every country to play on the presidential course in Longview and dance in the grand ballroom. And on that course—or in that ballroom—we'll negotiate the best trade deals that have ever been seen.

"I'm not that into negotiating right now. I negotiated a deal with Covfefe just yesterday morning. Great deal. Got back all the people who have gone missing over the past hundred years or more. Just a misunderstanding. Except criminals. We aren't getting back any criminals. The criminals are all being given a permanent home in space. Permanent. We'll just be telling other countries what we want from them. Not going to waste time on negotiations. Come and play golf, ball in our room, and give us what we want.

"Now as a part of our deal, there will be Covfefe—that's what the aliens call themselves—Covfefe will be seen here in America. Don't be shocked. They're safe. They are the only immigrants we'll be allowing into our country from now on. They'll make our country safer. They'll be watching for corruption and waste in local governments, just like they are on a national scale. It needs to be cleaned up now. This is what we wanted all along. Good common sense government.

"And if you think you can take your second amendment rights to just shoot at will, expect you'll get shot at, too. Whole bunch of people in Washington yesterday discovered bullets fly two ways. No reason for us to test that theory again.

"Nobody's taking away anybody's guns. We might need them if things get corrupt again. Things aren't corrupt now. Nobody's going to take away our God-given right to bear arms. Guns are God's way of pointing us to the righteous path. In fact, I'm striking a deal to release a new gold-plated nine-millimeter handgun with the presidential seal on it. Each one will be numbered and signed by yours truly. That will be an arm worth bearing. Plan to buy yours for just $1,999.99.

"Now, there will be some changes because our alien friends are more advanced than we are. You can expect changes to come, and if you just let yourself go, you'll enjoy them.

"Here beside me is Janelle Cummbridge, our new secretary of sex education. That's right. Our science is going to change because alien science is so much more advanced. We won't be talking about global warming again for hundreds of years. Science is all going to change.

"Beyond the basic principles of math and English and communication, the most important thing everyone here needs to learn is sex. I said that word out loud. If you have to go cover your ears because I said a bad word, goodbye. If you are a liberal who thinks everyone needs to be protected from sex, goodbye to you, too. It doesn't make a difference if you are liberal or conservative, you got here through sex. The whole human race is here because of sex. We should all learn to enjoy it more.

"I'm good at sex. Probably the best at sex of anyone. I've probably had more sex than anyone else and I plan to have a lot more. I'll even have sex with Janelle to prove our commitment to sex. So, everyone should subscribe to the channels for sex education that we've established. Janelle will teach you what you need to know.

"I was on the phone to the Russian and Chinese presidents this morning. They thought they could intimidate us because we are changing our country and getting rid of the communists and fascists. I set them straight. I told them they needed to have more sex. I didn't mince any words. I don't even know how to mince words. Is that some kind of pie filling? Minced words? Someone fix me one of those minced word pies so I can taste it. I didn't mince words with the Chinese or the Russians. We have the greatest ally we could ever need and they are watching overhead. They'll know if you try anything. We're putting a seventy-five percent tariff on everything imported from those two countries until further notice. That's over and above any existing tariffs. We won't mince words with them.

"In the next few months, I'm going to completely stamp out abortion. And we won't be doing it with any new laws. We've got too many laws right now. That's why we need a new constitution and fewer laws. I'm not going to pass any laws against abortion. In the future, nobody will get pregnant who doesn't want to have children. You can ask me how we're going to do that. Well, we've got an idea for a plan and within the next nine months, there won't be any unwanted pregnancies, no matter who you have sex with or how often. It's okay if we reduce the population a little. Too many people now. And we'll stop immigration, except our allies Covfefe. We'll have more sex and fewer babies and no abortions.

"Let me tell you about how we'll get rid of vaccines. Nobody likes vaccines. Nobody likes to get vaccines. And why should they? We'll eliminate vaccines. Vaccines keep people from getting certain diseases. You know what they don't do? They don't eliminate the disease. That's right. When people stopped getting measles vaccines, they started getting measles. Why? Because the vaccine didn't eliminate measles. If someone keeps beating you up, you don't go hide from them. You don't put on armor and a doctor's mask. You go out and eliminate the bully. You deport him. Make him into dogfood. That's what we'll do with measles. Eliminate the disease and stop having to hide and armor ourselves with a vaccine.

"I can't go into all the changes we're going to make in America. Too many changes to talk about. We'd be here all day. Probably tomorrow, too. And we still wouldn't get through all the changes we're going to make. So, I want to announce the newly created Ambassador to Covfefe to help us navigate the tricky waters of our new alliance. Please welcome Ambassadors Cece and Austin Warden. First thing they did last night was negotiate renovations to the new presidential palace. Our new head of security is Oswald Kennedy, known and beloved by people here in Longview, Kansas.

"You know what I found out when I got here to Longview? This is where food comes from. Lots of food. Enough food to feed everyone in the country. Maybe everyone in the world! More food than you've ever seen. There's no reason for anyone to be hungry. We have a plan to feed everyone. A great plan. You'll be amazed at how everyone gets fed when we start this plan.

"Roads? Why would we need roads when we can all have flying cars? And they won't use fossil fuel or disrupt the power grid. It will be great. We'll have flying cars and doctors on the television and robots who do the housecleaning. It'll be like the Flotsams. When we have all that, we won't need as many people so it's okay if we lose some of the population. We'll have everything and everyone we need.

"America the beautiful will be America the great. It will be more beautiful and more great than it's ever been. We're just getting started. We drained the swamp in Washington and we'll drain it in every state capital in the country. If it didn't get drained yesterday, it will be today or tomorrow. And we saw all the writhing slimy creatures of the swamp exposed to the light of day. We scooped them all up and got rid of them. Don't ask where. They'll never bother us again.

"That's all I've got to say right now. My wife just landed out at the airport and I need to get back to the presidential palace and fuck her. That's right. Sex is what makes the world go round. Sex is patriotic. Sex is fun. Go home. Go home and have sex! And Happy Halloween."

THERE WERE SOME really happy teens in Longview when they returned to high school on Monday. It was as if the whole 'Naked in School' universe had suddenly moved to Longview. And right in the middle of it was the new Secretary of Sex Education, Janelle Cummbridge.

As for the rest of Longview, there didn't seem to be much change. People still met up at Sarah Lee's Diner for coffee in the morning. They discussed the affairs of the day, sometimes different than 'affairs' implied before. Bert Beeson found himself in demand by a number of newly liberated woman—and a few men. He was proud to be the mayor of Longview.

And Little Johnny… Well, he got his own special education at the hands of his classmate, skinny Becca, who thought his alien costume was the coolest she'd ever seen.

The End

A Probing Interview with Author Devon Layne

THERE WAS REALLY no one who could get as deep in this interview as Devon's alter ego, Nathan Everett. Since this is associated with a novella subtitled "A Political Satire, in which everyone gets screwed," it seems appropriate to explore what it means to the author.

Nathan Everett: Devon, I'm surprised to find you releasing *Alienable Rights* as a Signature Edition. First of all, it's a very short book—a novella. Secondly, it is certainly not one of your highest rated books. What is the motivation?

Devon Layne: Obviously, it surprises me as much as it does you. It was a rather sudden inspiration. I doubt anyone will buy this little book, but I wanted a copy on my shelf to prove that I spoke up, even when it wasn't popular. Which sounds a whole lot more noble than it is. It is one of my lowest rated stories, pretty much tied with my 2024 Valentine story, *Carousel.* I think that says more about the readers than about the story itself, but I'm not going to blame ratings on anything other than the story.

NE: So, why? Why subject yourself to the kind of criticism you receive from stories like this? People don't like politics.

DL: Oh, I think people love politics. They love to be offended by other people's thoughts. Not so much by their actions. They really want to criticize what people think. That's sort of harmless and gets people's juices flowing. Just listening in restaurants, stage shows, airports, and such, I hear a non-stop conversations on politics. I even get caught up in such conversations with my good friend, Al, with whom I violently agree on most topics.

NE: One of your readers of *Forever Yours* reviewed the book on ZBookStore saying, "This was a decent book at first. It was fairly dry and pedantic, but pleasant… until it began to get political. I read as an escape from reality. If I wanted to read about politics, I wouldn't have chosen a science fiction book." Do you think people want to read about political things?

DL: No. We want to 'escape from reality.' But I don't think you can do that completely. Certainly not with what I write. Escapist literature still makes you think. What the reviewer was saying was simply, "I don't want to think." In which case, he should try meditation rather than science fiction. In fact, science fiction, which is one of the categories I'd include *Alienable Rights* in, is and has always been focused on making people think. If nothing else, think about what the world or the universe *could be*.

NE: You don't even *try* to keep that out of your writing.

DL: I don't think it's possible to keep every part of yourself out of your writing, as you well know from the books you've written. Everything about you is reflected in some way in what you write, even if it is only your fantasies. Here's the thing: If I wrote a book extolling the virtues of a mindset I was personally opposed to, that would come through. Somehow, I would expose what I believed the fallacies of that mindset are. In the interest of being fair, mind you.

I'll use a famous author as an example. Orson Scott Card wrote some incredible science fiction books. There was a hint of his faith in them, but the *Ender's Game* series was an intriguing conceptual series, born from the cold war and Card's belief in a universal union of all species. I loved the books. Eventually, however, Card moved further and further into expressing his Mormon beliefs in his writing, so much so that in his *Alvin Maker* series, I ended up putting the books aside because I didn't want to listen to him preach, even though the books were well-written. Perhaps that is what the reviewer of *Forever Yours* was really getting at.

Fundamentally, though, it is not possible to extract the author from the story. What you are, what you believe, and how you act will ultimately come through in the story. Every story. Every time.

NE: Do you think you were bludgeoning people with your politics in *Alienable Rights*?

DL: Yes! Definitely. You can't do satire and parody without bludgeoning people. That's what makes it satire. People won't get it if it's subtle. Why did I hit the presidential character so hard? It's just obvious to do so. I made up speeches for him regarding the aliens that sounded more like him than he does. Because it was a parody. Then I set about having the alien substitute parody him with all the reasons everything he'd promoted were actually good ideas. Get rid of vaccines because we get rid of the disease. Get rid of education because we only need sex education. Get rid of roads because we'll have flying cars. And go home and have more sex. We'll get rid of abortion by getting rid of unwanted pregnancy.

I've done this once before. Sadly, under the same president. He's just so easy to parody. When I wrote *Adams' Apples*, we were just becoming lost in the COVID pandemic. Personally, I was trapped in a nearly empty RV park in Phar, Texas. I couldn't leave because there was a travel ban and none of the places to stay were open to new arrivals. I was miserable and isolated for six weeks. So, I wrote about a virus that sterilized all the men on earth, except the one who was in orbit when the virus struck. Then I just started making shit up about how people would respond to that. Every day, I made new stuff up and the next day I would read something even more ridiculous in the news feed that was really happening. Drink bleach? Really? Well, a combination of ammonia and vinegar proved to be the cure for the virus in my book. I just let it run.

NE: And *Adams' Apples* was not highly praised either.

DL: No. The people drinking bleach didn't like it.

NE: Do you think you'll be writing more political satire in the future?

DL: The question is whether or not I'll be writing in the future. My writing is getting better with each book I release. However, it is possible—like with Card—my opinions are permeating my stories more heavily than ever. We'll see how people respond to the time travel story coming up next.

NE: It worries me to think you might not write in the future. Any last words?

DL: That does sound final! I'm not dead yet. I'll include as my last words here the same ones I put in the front of the book:

> *This is a work of adult fiction. This book contains content of an adult nature. This includes explicit sexual content and characters whose beliefs may be contrary to your religious, political, or world view—I hope. The content is inappropriate, and in some cases, illegal for readers under the age of 18.*

If you aren't able to read words that may be contrary to your religious, political, or world view, you aren't adult enough to read my books.